*"I'd like to s _____ l.
His voice was r _____ n
her spine. "If y _____"*

"Not at all," Rachel said. She was surprised that her own voice was quiet and almost steady, belying her inner turmoil.

He boldly stared back at her, his gaze traveling over her slender body. He'd thought her beautiful before, but after the birth of a child and so many years, she wondered if he still found her attractive. In the darkness she thought she saw his mouth curve into a sensuous smile, saw his hand begin to lift, as if to caress her.

Whatever fire had burned between them long ago, whatever current of charged desire had pulled them together, the attraction was still just as strong . . . in fact, it seemed even more potent. Her body ached for his touch, cried out for his embrace.

She looked up at him and was stunned that even in the shadowy night she could see the raw hunger in his eyes. The chasm of unspoken words that lay between them was still waiting to be crossed. . . .

WHAT ARE *LOVESWEPT* ROMANCES?

They are stories of true romance and touching emotion. We believe those two very important ingredients are constants in our highly sensual and very believable stories in the *LOVESWEPT* line. Our goal is to give you, the reader, stories of consistently high quality that may sometimes make you laugh, sometimes make you cry, but are always fresh and creative and contain many delightful surprises within their pages.

Most romance fans read an enormous number of books. Those they truly love, they keep. Others may be traded with friends and soon forgotten. We hope that each *LOVESWEPT* romance will be a treasure—a "keeper." We will always try to publish

LOVE STORIES YOU'LL NEVER FORGET
BY AUTHORS YOU'LL ALWAYS REMEMBER

The Editors

LOVESWEPT® • 184

Anne and Ed Kolaczyk
Sultry Nights

BANTAM BOOKS
TORONTO • NEW YORK • LONDON • SYDNEY • AUCKLAND

SULTRY NIGHTS

A Bantam Book / March 1987

*LOVESWEPT® and the wave device are registered
trademarks of Bantam Books, Inc. Registered in U.S. Patent
and Trademark Office and elsewhere.*

*If you would be interested in receiving protective vinyl
covers for your Loveswept books, please write to this address
for information:*

*Loveswept
Bantam Books
P.O. Box 985
Hicksville, NY 11802*

ISBN 0-553-21812-3

Published simultaneously in the United States and Canada

*Bantam Books are published by Bantam Books, Inc. Its trade-
mark, consisting of the words "Bantam Books" and the por-
trayal of a rooster, is Registered in U.S. Patent and Trademark
Office and in other countries. Marca Registrada. Bantam
Books, Inc., 666 Fifth Avenue, New York, New York 10103.*

PRINTED IN THE UNITED STATES OF AMERICA

O   0 9 8 7 6 5 4 3 2 1

To Suzette, Julie, and Kate.
Monday nights aren't the same
without you.

One

Rachel leaned on the stone wall and gazed out over the bluff. Below her was the Mississippi River and beyond that was Wisconsin. To her right and behind her was Dubuque, the city that had been her home so long ago, but she chose not to look that way. Not yet.

Instead, she gazed out over the river, remembering the nights when she and Ben would slip up here to Eagle Point Park. In the safety of the darkness, they would explore the wonder that they had discovered between them. The gentlest touch of his large hands would turn her body to fire, and their need would be so strong that neither of them could think of anything but the other.

She felt rather than heard the presence behind her. "This is a neat place, Mom. It has to be the local lover's lane, right?"

Rachel turned to her fourteen-year-old daughter. A red and black MEET ME IN ST. LOUIS T-shirt hid

Laura's burgeoning figure, hanging so loose and low on her hips that it nearly covered the red knitted shorts she wore. Her feet were bare, leather sandals dangling from her hand.

"Lover's lane?" Rachel repeated, her gaze going back to the river. "I didn't think anybody used that phrase anymore."

"Come on, Mom," Laura said. She was not so easily put off. "There had to be a reason why you wanted to stop here before we went on to Grandma and Grandpa's." A sly smile appeared on her face. "I'll bet you had some terrific times here and couldn't wait to see the old place."

Rachel turned away from the river. The rough edges of the stone wall pressed against her back as she looked at the oak trees towering over them. She had a sudden vision of the park on a summer night, the stars peeking through the leaves of the trees and gentle breezes caressing the darkness. Of love so strong that she thought she would die with wanting.

"My life when I was growing up was very different from yours now," she said to her daughter. "I never had half the freedom you have."

Laura sighed. "Come on, Mom. You must have snuck up here sometimes. Why else would you want to come here first?"

"How about to say good-bye?"

"To what?" Laura looked astonished.

Rachel laughed. Her depression had grown with each mile she had driven, but at least she hadn't let it show. "Once Grandma and Grandpa move, I won't be coming back to Dubuque. I had some happy times here."

"That's not what you usually say," Laura pointed out. She took off her sunglasses, perching them on top of her head. "You always made it sound like this was the worst place in the world to grow up."

"So I exaggerated," Rachel said with a laugh, then sobered as little bits of the past smiled at her. "But being the daughter of a college president wasn't easy. It was like living under a microscope most of the time. I felt as if everyone were watching me and waiting to report my smallest slip to my father."

Was it any wonder that she had flown into Ben's arms? she mused. She felt the corners of her mouth twitch. Flown indeed. Like a canary fleeing the confinement and safety of the cage for the freedom and danger of the meadow. She and Laura started toward their car.

"So what was his name?" Laura asked.

"What was whose name?" Rachel asked, taking the car keys from the pocket of her navy shorts.

"The guy you were up here with."

Rachel opened her side of the car and got in. The vinyl seat scorched her bare legs. She shouldn't have parked the car on this side of the lot, she thought, or else she should be wearing a skirt instead of shorts. She hoped it wasn't an omen of disaster approaching, but this whole trip had her strangely unnerved.

"Was he my father?" Laura asked.

The car seemed stifling suddenly, and the car keys clattered to the floor. "Your father?" Rachel repeated.

"Well, since you went to live with Aunt Mary

when you were pregnant, you must have known my father here in Dubuque."

"Yes." Her voice was stiff and dry, and there was no reason for her to clam up. Except that everything seemed different today. She no longer felt like a thirty-one-year-old woman, but like that terrified girl who had been shipped off to her mother's cousin to have her baby amid strangers. Rachel felt around on the floor until she found the keys, then started the car. Soon she and Laura were out of the park.

"I just wondered if I was likely to meet him," Laura went on thoughtfully. "It never really bothered me before, not knowing who my father was. David was so great that I usually forgot that I was already four when you married him."

"He loved you like his own daughter."

Laura nodded and turned to stare out the window. It was more than a year since David's fatal heart attack, but Rachel knew how Laura felt. It still hurt her too. She didn't need to add to Laura's pain by refusing to answer simple questions.

"You don't have to view every man over thirty with suspicion," she said briskly. "You won't meet your father here." She stopped at the light at Dodge Street and turned right. "He was only visiting some relatives for the summer. He was gone before I even knew I was pregnant."

"He never knew about me." Laura's voice was quiet but controlled.

"No."

"Couldn't you have tried to contact him through his relatives?"

Rachel bit her lip. They'd been to Dubuque before, just last month, when Rachel's father had had the stroke. But things had been hectic then, and the other trips had been filled with Christmas plans or birthday doings. This trip was different; it had such a feeling of finality about it. She should have expected Laura to start asking questions.

"I got his address and did write," Rachel admitted slowly. "But he never answered."

"So maybe he did know about me." Laura sounded suddenly like a hurt little girl and Rachel reached over to squeeze her hand.

"No, he didn't know about you," she assured her daughter. "He would have come back, I know he would have. I don't think my letter ever reached him."

In her mind she saw Ben: his dark unruly hair, the striking blue-green eyes that had possessed her with his love, the tall figure that ought to have been ungainly but was capable of such tenderness. He would have come back had he known, she told herself as she had so many times before. He wouldn't have left her to face things alone. But the memory of their last argument still lingered, and so did the doubts. They were hers to live with, though, not Laura's.

"Are you ever going to tell me his name?" Laura asked.

Rachel turned to look at her daughter. She had grown accustomed to seeing Ben's blue-green tiger eyes staring back at her, but thanks to Laura's new tinted contacts, her daughter's eyes were violet now. "Maybe someday."

"But not today." There was amused resignation in Laura's voice.

Rachel turned back to the road. "No. Not today." After a moment, she went on. "His name won't mean anything to you when I do tell you. He's not a celebrity."

"But I can't find him without his name."

"Find him?" Rachel was startled and glanced quickly toward the girl. Laura had leaned her head back against the car seat, an expression of wistfulness and longing on her face. "What do you mean, find him?"

"Just what I said. I think that someday I would like to find him. Maybe he'd be happy to know he has a daughter."

"It might also come as a shock," Rachel warned.

Laura shrugged. "Before David died, I always thought of him as my father, but now that he's gone, I've been thinking more and more of my other father. Wouldn't it be wonderful to find him and have us be a real family?"

From the corner of her eye, Rachel could see the hopeful look on her daughter's face. How could this levelheaded, mature girl be cherishing such unrealistic dreams? "Honey, he could be married with a family of his own by now. He might not even be alive. And even if he is, how would you ever find him? Look in the phone books of all the major cities? What if his number's unlisted?"

Rachel knew he wasn't in the St. Louis phone book, because she had checked one dreary day not long after David's death. She had wondered then if he might just have an unlisted number. It had been a frightening thought: that her Ben was only a few miles away, and she'd never know.

She had told herself he was in her mind only because of the pain of losing David. It was natural that she should remember the other love she had lost. She had resolved not to think about Ben again and she hadn't. Until her father had had the stroke and was replaced as president of the college.

Now she and Laura had come to help her parents move. Along with her childhood home, she was also losing the home of so many special memories. The park where she and Ben had met in the sweetness of the night. The gazebo where she had dreamed away her summer afternoons with thoughts of him.

"Do Grandma and Grandpa know who he is?" Laura asked suddenly.

"No." Rachel's voice was strained. They had known Ben, of course, for he was the academic dean's nephew and had been staying with Dean Healey that summer. But she had refused, even in the face of her father's raging anger, to tell them Ben was the father of her child.

She had met Ben at a faculty picnic and had been drawn to him immediately. In his gentle blue-green eyes she had seen the sensitive, caring person he really was beneath his outrageous clothes and defiant behavior. Still hurting from his parents' death five years earlier when he had been thirteen, Ben lived wildly in an effort to deal with the world. She had wanted to soothe his hurts and ease his pain, but soon had found something stronger that drew them together, a need, a wanting that was greater than reason itself.

She had been terrified her father would forbid her to see Ben, as he had forbidden her to see other boys who were "too old," "too wild," or somehow lacking in his eyes. What she had felt for Ben was so special, so strong, that she had wanted to treasure it by herself. When they had started meeting, she had persuaded him to keep those meetings secret, under the cover of night and deep in the park, even though he hadn't liked it.

He loved her, he had said, and wasn't ashamed of it. He didn't like sneaking around behind her father's back. But she had known what would happen if he went to her parents: it would be good-bye Ben. She wouldn't have been able to bear that happening, although it had happened in the end. He had gone off to college, refusing even to write to her unless he could do so openly. She had been certain he would weaken and waited for him to write first. When she finally did write, it had been too late. She had always assumed he'd thrown her letter out without even reading it.

Rachel automatically turned into a parking lot and stopped, then was rather surprised to find they had arrived. The hot August air pressed down on her, making it hard for her to breathe. Where had this overwhelming uneasiness come from?

"I love this place," Laura said. "It looks like something out of Mr. Chips."

Rachel looked at the bucolic scene. Ivy-covered brick buildings were set amid towering oaks, and behind the college library stood the red brick house that had been her home. Everything was serene and peaceful. This was a Hollywood director's dream of a small college campus, and hardly reason for the tension that was knotting up her stomach.

Laura was already climbing out of the car, and Rachel followed reluctantly. Why did she find the heat so oppressive? There never was a breeze here in August, and it hadn't ever bothered her so before.

They got their suitcases from the trunk and carried them to the large, solid house with the porch stretching across its front. Even the cracks in the sidewalk evoked haunting memories for Rachel. She'd learned to roller-skate on this sidewalk. She'd sat on these wide cement steps to put on her skates, tightening the clamps with the skate key she wore around her neck on a red ribbon. In the beginning, she always tripped on that one big crack where the sidewalk curved around the fir tree, then had learned to step over it without losing her balance. What a triumph that had been.

Nothing ever seemed to change here, she thought. Red petunias would line the walk forever and the grass would always be brown in August from the heat. She felt as if she were caught in a time warp. She hadn't really ever left. If she looked down, she'd see the skate key dangling from its ribbon.

The front door was standing open and she peered inside. "Mom?" she called, but her voice just echoed in the hallway.

"Maybe she's in the garden," Laura said, and stepped into the hall.

Rachel followed, setting the suitcases down just inside the door. By the time she straightened up, Laura was halfway down the hall to the kitchen. "Gran?" she was calling as she disappeared behind the door.

Rachel sighed and walked forward, her footsteps swallowed up by the dark green carpet. It was strange to think of someone else living in this house, someone else typing in the office, some other little girl learning to skate on her sidewalk. It hadn't been her home for years now, but, in a way, it always would be.

Instead of following Laura, Rachel opened the door to her father's office. The room was large, but not as overpowering as she had thought as a child. She walked slowly to the middle of the room. The same desk was there and the same leather chair. Drawn to the chair, she ran her hand along its back, but its warmth was from the sun, not from her father. His pipe stand was gone from the shelf where he'd always kept it; a digital clock radio was in its place. By the window was a desktop computer. Open boxes lay scattered about the floor, books spilling out and ready to fill the empty shelves. It wasn't her father's office anymore. The new president was obviously already using it.

Rachel felt as if she were intruding and had turned to go, when a man appeared in the doorway. She sensed his presence, his nearness, even before she took in his broad shoulders and blue-green eyes. Her stomach went plummeting to her feet while her heart leaped into her throat.

Large tiger eyes framed with thick, dark lashes.

Eyes that had told her of love when words hadn't been enough. Eyes that had darkened with passion when she had lain in his arms. They were Laura's eyes now. Was she dreaming? Rachel wondered. Had she conjured up a vision from her sadness at losing her home?

"Rachel?"

No, he wasn't a dream. His voice was both stronger and softer, but the same in so many ways. His mouth curved into a smile that still had power over her, and she had a sudden vivid hunger to feel those lips pressed against hers. Her eyes drank him in: his hair, still dark and unruly but short now, his clothes neat and "establishment."

He took a step into the room. She wanted to ask why he was here. She wanted to say something witty and cool, something devastatingly modern and liberated, but after a few seconds of inarticulate gulping, she would have settled for any sort of coherent sound.

Her mother came into the office just then, a welcoming expression on her face as she quickly embraced Rachel. "Oh, honey, it's good to see you. I'd been watching all morning for you and then the phone had to ring when you pulled up. I take it you've met Dr. Healey, the new president of the college."

"New president?" Rachel repeated. This had to be a joke. Ben wasn't really here. She *had* been caught in a time warp. She was sixteen again. Her body, warming with unexpected desire, told her so.

"You might even remember him," her mother

continued. "Ben came out one summer and stayed with his uncle, Dean Healey."

"That was a long time ago, Jessica," Ben said to Rachel's mother.

But was it? Rachel asked herself. His eyes were ever so gently awakening more than just memories. Her lips remembered the feel of him and yearned to know him again; her hands ached for the chance to touch and explore. She was an adult now, a mature, responsible person with control over her feelings and actions. Yet under Ben's tender gaze she felt like a teenager again, wild and reckless for love. Hungry for the taste of his passion. She took a deep breath and willed herself back to adulthood.

"It's good to see you again, Dr. Healey," she finally said. She couldn't allow herself to fall apart under his gaze, she thought. "It's been a long time."

"Ben," he corrected her gently. "Yes, it's been too long."

What did that mean? she wondered. Had he missed her? But these were not questions she chose to ask, even of herself. She preferred the safety that came with leaving the past in the past, and rushed into other avenues of distraction.

"I hope you don't think I was prying," she said quickly, waving her hand about the office. "I was just looking for my mother and had no idea you were already moving your things in."

"The only thoughts that crossed my mind were pleasant ones," he assured her.

"Oh?" Confusion reigned in her heart as some emotion flared suddenly in his tiger eyes. Her sense of safety fled. Memories of their past, of touching and longing and splendor, washed over her, tugging at her good sense.

"I was pleasantly surprised to find you here," he said. "This has been your home for a long time. You mustn't feel that's changed just because I've got a few boxes in a corner."

"Actually, she was never allowed in here much as a child," Jessica said with a laugh. "Neither of us were, so I don't know why she came in here to look for me."

"Mom," Rachel cried in mock dismay. "You make it sound like I was snooping around."

Her mother just laughed again and turned to Ben. "Why don't you join us for dinner tonight?" she asked. "It'll be a simple meal, but we'd enjoy your company."

"The pleasure will be all mine," he said, but his eyes found Rachel's, stirring her senses into bewilderment and leaving her with an overwhelming need to flee.

"I'd like to freshen up, Mother, and say hello to Father," she said quickly. She needed time to breathe freely, to push those hungers back into the past, where they belonged, and settle the quivering in her stomach. The sudden padding of Laura's bare feet in the hallway caused Rachel's panic to double. She needed time to think. "What rooms have you given us?" she asked her mother, even as she edged toward the door.

"The east bedrooms as usual." Her mother frowned at her, looking as if she were ready to scold sixteen-year-old Rachel for being rude.

"I'll look forward to seeing you at dinner," Rachel said to Ben, then sped from the room before he had time to answer. She met Laura in the hallway. Laura, her darling, wonderful daughter, who had just been wondering who her father was.

"Let's take the suitcases upstairs, sweetheart," Rachel said. "Then we can peek in on Grandpa."

Laura tilted her head to the side, trying to see into the office. "Is somebody in there with Grandma?"

Yes, your father. Rachel's heart threatened to stop altogether. Why had she come back? She should have known it would be a mistake. But could seeing Ben, could resting in the gentleness of his smile once more, really be a mistake?

She tried again. "Yes," she said. "Dr. Healey, the new president, is here." She was surprised at how cool and detached she sounded. When had she become so good at dissembling? "But you'll meet him at dinner. Your grandmother has invited him to eat with us."

That thought was enough to make Rachel's stomach churn, but Laura just dismissed Ben with a wrinkle of her nose and bent down to pick up her suitcase.

"Great," she said. "Our first day here and we're saddled with a stuffy old fogy."

Oh, if only the new president were just that, Rachel thought.

Two

Ben put the last of the books on the shelf, then finally looked at what he was doing. He frowned. What kind of arrangement was this? Textbooks mixed in with novels and technical journals. Where had his mind been?

That wasn't too hard to figure out. It had been lingering on a pair of blue eyes and a slight figure that still had the power to turn his body to fire. He pulled some books off the shelf and began to rearrange them.

He had known Rachel was coming back, of course. Jessica had talked of little else for the past week and, in her excitement, had answered questions he hadn't known to ask. How strange it had been, after so many years, to hear of Rachel again. Not that she had ever been forgotten. Still, it was hard to imagine her as a wife and mother, that willful girl with deeply hidden passion. To think of her smiling at her husband over the breakfast table, driving her daughter's Brownie troop around in their station wagon, and growing older. She must have changed, he had decided a few days ago. Her haunting beauty must have faded into quiet attractiveness, just as surely as her golden hair must have dulled with time.

But he'd been wrong. One look into those deep blue eyes and he'd known that vulnerable, wistful girl was still there. He'd seen pain in her eyes, too, and that saddened him. He'd known her husband had died last year, Jessica had told him that, but he hadn't wanted to see Rachel still hurting.

"Oh, Ben," Jessica said from the doorway. "We'll be eating in a few minutes if you're ready to join us."

"Gladly," he said, and put down the books he was holding. How long had the woman been standing there? he wondered. Long enough to see his inability to function?

Together they walked out into the hallway. It was the same hallway Ben had been through for days now as he moved his things into the office, but today it felt different. Rachel was home.

"It was good to see Rachel again," he said, his thoughts coming out unexpectedly in words.

"Yes. I wish she and Laura lived closer."

They entered the parlor. Rachel wasn't there yet, and he was strongly aware of his disappointment.

"Would you like a glass of sherry before dinner?" Jessica asked.

"If you're having one."

While she poured the drinks, he wandered over to the bookshelves lining the back wall. A montage of snapshots caught his eye and he studied it. They were pictures of Rachel growing from dimpled childhood to the graceful young woman who had owned his heart that summer. He stared at the last teenage picture. Remarkably, the camera had caught the Rachel he had known. He could see the yearning in her eyes, the touch of fire waiting to be set free, the promise of passion. Her eyes had captured him first that summer, and had haunted him since.

"Ben."

He spun around. Rachel was holding his drink out to him, not her mother. They were alone in the parlor.

"Mother went to see if dinner was ready," Rachel explained.

He nodded and sipped at the sherry. Her eyes could still disturb him.

"So how have you been?" she asked.

It was such a normal question, such an ordinary one, he thought. Why should he feel disgruntled?

"Fine," he said. His voice seemed overly loud in the small room, and he tried to turn down the volume. "Been busy, you know."

She nodded and turned away, staring out the window at something more fascinating than him.

"How about yourself?" he asked, not very cleverly.

She turned from the window, seeming almost startled to see him there. "Oh, I've been fine too." She sipped at her drink, her eyes not meeting his. "Been busy too."

"Your mother told me about your husband's heart attack last year. I'm sorry."

She nodded, but her glance just flickered toward

him for a moment, then she looked away. "We miss him, Laura and I. He was a good man."

There seemed to be nothing else to say, but Ben told himself that shouldn't really surprise him. They'd known each other for only two months many years ago. What would there be to say after all that time?

"Dinner's ready," Jessica announced from the doorway, then frowned. "Where's Laura? Isn't she down yet?"

"She—" Rachel began, only to be interrupted by a bundle of blond energy that flew into the room.

"Sorry I'm late," the girl said. She was a younger Rachel, Ben saw instantly, but was more carefree, more effervescent than Rachel had ever been. "I stopped to see Grandpa first."

"Laura," Rachel scolded gently. "Most people wear their shoes, not take them for a walk like a dog."

Laura looked down at the sandals swinging from her hand and giggled. "Sorry, Mom. I forgot." She slipped her feet into them even as Jessica took her arm.

"Ben, this young hoyden is my granddaughter, Laura." The twinkle in Jessica's eye belied any reprimand her words might have held. "Laura, this is Dr. Healey, the new president of the college."

Laura shook his hand politely. "How do you do?" she said. Her violet eyes stared up into his with mischief, then she turned back to her mother. "You were wrong, Mom. He's not an old fogy at all."

"Laura!" Rachel gasped, her face turning red. "I never said that!"

Laura just grinned. "I know. I did. But you didn't tell me I was wrong."

Ben laughed at the girl's outrageousness. She was charming, a young lady about to blossom into a woman, and surprisingly self-confident and mature for a girl her age. Somehow he had expected her to look more like a child. How old was she? Eleven? Twelve?

Jessica was shooing them into the dining room and his gaze fell upon Rachel. What had she been like at eleven or twelve? he wondered. Had she been as brash and as sure of herself as her daughter was? No, he thought not. It had been Rachel's vulnerability that had drawn him, that still drew him. There was an uncertainty about her, a sense of quiet struggling that awoke all sorts of protective feelings in him. Feelings that should have died years ago, when they'd argued and he'd left.

"There'll just be the four of us at dinner," Jessica said. "Robert's on a special diet and doesn't come down for meals yet."

"How is he feeling?" Ben asked as they all sat down. "I've been hoping to meet with him soon about college business."

"Yes, he knows that you're waiting and it shouldn't be much longer," Jessica assured him as if she hadn't been saying the same thing for a week.

"He was in good spirits when Laura and I saw him this afternoon," Rachel said. "He seems to be recovering quite well, though he's not happy about having to leave the school."

She broke off as the college student assigned to help out in their kitchen brought the food in and served them. There was pot roast with potatoes and carrots and freshly baked rolls.

"So . . . Ben," Rachel said, hesitating slightly at the use of his first name. "Tell us, is there a Mrs. Healey?"

He wanted to read her eyes, to see if any hidden message lay there for him, but she was looking down at her plate, eating with apparent ease. Did she still treasure the dreams they had spun in the darkness, the future they had planned to conquer? he wondered. But how could she have? She had abandoned those dreams herself.

"No, there's no Mrs. Healey," he said. "I've never seemed to have the time to settle down." For some reason, he needed to show her that he hadn't taken those dreams seriously either, that he hadn't given them any thought at all since he'd left Dubuque all those years ago. "For a while I was too busy traveling, seeing new places. I spent quite some time in the Orient and in the Mediterranean." With the Marines actually, but he saw no reason to add that little detail.

"How lucky for you," Rachel said.

Her voice was polite and gracious, yet he could have sworn the temperature of it had dropped.

"Yeah," Laura agreed, but with warmer emotion. "We've been to Chicago twice, Kansas City once, and Dubuque. When I grow up, I'm going to good places too."

Ben laughed. "There's lots of good places waiting for you."

"You must find Dubuque quiet after such an exciting life," Rachel said. She was buttering a roll with great concentration.

"I've always loved it here," he said, answering the challenge he heard in her voice. "Some of my fondest memories are of Dubuque. I was glad to come back."

Her cheeks reddened slightly and her gaze remained on her plate as Jessica passed around the platter of pot roast for second helpings.

"Did you go to school here at the college?" Laura asked. "I'd like to do that at my junior high, come back in ten years as the principal. First thing I'd do is fire Mr. Turner."

"Sound like fun, but no," Ben said as he helped himself to more meat. "I was here visiting relatives one summer years ago. That's when I first met your mother and grandparents."

Laura frowned at him. "Oh?"

"You were lucky any of us would talk to you," Jessica said, chuckling. "The way you dressed! Why, I can still remember those cutoffs and strange sandals you used to wear."

"I didn't think my clothes bothered anyone as much as my motorcycle did," he said. "Uncle John nearly had a heart attack when he saw that."

Jessica laughed. "I can imagine!"

"Father forbade motorcycles on campus after you left," Rachel said. He looked at her, but she wouldn't meet his eyes. "Though he had to amend the rule to allow motorbikes now that they've become so popular."

"I guess I'd better keep my checkered past a secret then," Ben said, "or we might be overrun with Harley-Davidson's."

Rachel gave him a vague smile; Laura gave him none at all. The girl's brow was furrowed in thought, her lips tight with anger. Why? he wondered.

"All teenagers go through a rebellious stage," Jessica said, dragging his attention from Laura. "Maybe yours was just a little more visible than most."

"I did have a hard couple of years there," he admitted. "After my parents died in a plane crash, I was ready to fight the world."

"Or at least Dubuque," Rachel added.

He smiled at her, but her eyes didn't smile back. "I wasn't really thrilled with the family's custom of passing me around every summer," he said. "I guess I let everyone know it." Except that summer had been different for him. Rachel had soothed so much of his hurt, his anger at the world. How could someone who had done so much for him be so distant now?

"Robert was glad there were no students around for you to corrupt," Jessica said.

Ben's smile turned sad. "Maybe that's why he's refusing to see me now."

Jessica patted his hand. "Just give him time," she said. "It's not you personally. It's just hard to leave a place you've given your life to. At this time last year he would have been getting ready for the new semester, planning out the English literature class he always taught, and working on his programs for minority students. Now he just sits and remembers."

"I need to settle some things soon though," Ben said. "Classes start at the end of the month."

"He knows you're waiting," Jessica said. "He

loves the college too much to let it suffer because of his stubbornness."

"Grandpa's not stubborn," Laura said. She was surprisingly vehement. "He's a sweetheart."

"Honey—" Rachel began.

Jessica stepped in. "Yes, he's a sweetheart, but he can also be a stubborn old goat."

Laura looked close to tears, but said nothing as the college student came back in to clear the table, bringing with her a pie for dessert.

"I'll cut Grandpa a piece and eat mine upstairs with him," Laura announced as she jumped to her feet.

Jessica's disturbed glance went from the student clearing the table to Rachel, then over to her granddaughter, standing at the sideboard.

"Laura, maybe your grandfather's already had his dessert," Rachel said softly.

Ben saw Laura's hand tremble as she sliced the pie. Was she angry? he wondered. Hurt at what she took as insults to her grandfather? Making her stay would serve no purpose.

"Even if he has had dessert," Ben said, "I'd be willing to bet he'd agree to another piece in such delightful company." He gave Laura a conspiratorial smile and got a frosty glare in return. No one spoke as she marched from the room.

Through the dining room window Rachel watched Ben walk away from the house until his broad shoulders disappeared in the darkness beyond the lights by the library. What a day this had been! As if coming back to say good-bye to her childhood wasn't enough, her past was threatening to explode in her face. Even the evening air seemed oppressive, pregnant with the promise of a storm. Hearing of Ben's footloose, wandering life had only increased her sense of depression. Maybe when the storm passed her mood would lighten.

It had been nearly impossible to sit across the table from Ben during dinner. As an eighteen-year-old, he had been attractive, and certainly a potent temptation for a young girl. As a man, though, he was downright overwhelming. There was an aura of self-confidence about him, a confidence in himself as a person . . . and as a man. What women had he known in the past fifteen years? she couldn't help wondering. She wouldn't be surprised if there had been many, for there was something compelling in his tiger eyes, an intensity that would draw a woman irresistibly to him.

Or at least it drew Rachel. Every time she had dared glance at him during dinner, she had found him staring raptly at her, as if he could see into her heart. She had longed to be in his arms again just one more time. But that could never be.

The sound of footsteps roused her from her musings, and she turned to find her mother entering the room. Questions, fears, warred to come out. "Why won't Dad see Ben?" she asked.

"Stubbornness," her mother said with affection. "In spite of Laura's firm conviction, your father is stubborn."

Rachel smiled, more because it was expected of her than because she wanted to. "Is that the only reason?"

Her mother looked puzzled. "What other reason would he have?"

How about anger at the man who had gotten his daughter pregnant? Rachel asked silently.

"Robert just can't bear to meet the man who's taking his place," Jessica went on. "This move is hurting your father very much."

"Yes, he's been here a long time." Rachel told herself she was worrying for no reason. Surely if anyone had found out that Ben was Laura's father, she would know. It wasn't like her own father to keep that a secret.

She and her mother went upstairs to find Laura and her grandfather sitting on the second floor porch. Light spilling from the bedroom windows spotlighted them.

Rachel sat down on a bench near them. "What are you two up to?"

"Watching the lightning," Robert said.

"Grandpa says we'll have a storm by midnight. He says you can smell the rain in the air."

Rachel looked out at the distant sky, remembering a similar night fifteen Augusts ago. She and Ben had huddled behind Science Hall. He had wanted her to go back home, but she had been certain, in spite of her father's predictions that night, too, that the storm wouldn't reach them until the early hours of the morning. It had caught them halfway to the park and Ben had been furious. She would catch cold, or worse, he said. And how could she sneak back into the house looking like a drowned rat? He should just come with her and talk to her father, tell him of their feelings, and ask to see her openly.

Laura's voice brought Rachel back to the present. "I think Grandpa could get a job as a TV weatherman."

"I'm not doing anything any Iowa farmer can't do," Robert said, but he squeezed Laura's hand in thanks nonetheless.

"The weatherman on the TV said the storm will pass north of us," Jessica pointed out.

"No," Laura said. "Grandpa says it'll rain for less than an hour and then blow over. It'll be wet out in the morning, but the weather will be a lot more pleasant."

"Oh?" Rachel asked.

"They don't believe me," Robert grumbled, leaning over and kissing Laura on the cheek. "They're just like the board of trustees here at the college. A man gets a little older and they say he can't do the job anymore. I think I'll turn in and hope that every one of those trustees gets caught in the rain."

"Dad!" Rachel protested, but Laura was faster.

"I still think you're the greatest, Gramps." She returned his kiss with a big hug. "And I'm going to prove it by making the best breakfast ever for you. I know how to make omelettes."

"You'd better check with the warden on that," he said, pulling himself up out of his chair.

Jessica chuckled. "Your grandfather's on a low cholesterol diet, sweetheart. It's good for his heart, if not for his disposition. Come down to the kitchen with me and I'll show you what there is."

"Okay." Laura kissed Rachel lightly on the cheek. "'Night, Mom."

"Good night, honey." Rachel kissed her back,

but wished she had some reason to make her stay. Or to sneak off with her. She had so much she wanted to ask her daughter. What had she thought of Ben? Why had she been so upset at the end of dinner? But Laura was following her grandmother into the house.

"Dr. Healey said to say good night to you," she called after Laura, but the girl only shrugged and let the screen door close behind her.

Ben's laughter, the kindness in his smile, those tiger eyes, all seemed to close in around Rachel. She got to her feet and leaned against the porch rail. Her father stood beside her and together they stared out at the jagged flashes of lightning dancing across the dark sky. The moments stretched into a lifetime.

"Not coming any closer," Rachel said.

"Around midnight," her father insisted. "It'll pour cats and dogs, but not for long."

Silence rolled in around them like the fog on a Scottish moor. The bolts of lightning twirled and danced like mating hummingbirds. A car's headlights split the night momentarily as someone turned onto a nearby side street, but soon there was darkness again. Just darkness and the distant rumble of the coming storm.

"Who was he, Rachel?" her father asked, his words splitting the silence as the lightning split the sky.

"Who was who?" She was puzzled and had the feeling she had missed part of the conversation.

"Laura's father."

The air grew more oppressive, or was it just his words that weighed heavily on her?

"It doesn't make any difference anymore," he said slowly. "Everybody's gone, and I will be, too, pretty soon. The life I built for us here in Dubuque is over, but before we leave I'd like to know."

Rachel leaned down, resting her arms against the railing. It was still faintly warm from the sun, but she felt, instead, Ben's warmth. She saw the boy he had been, caring and comforting and ever so tender. She heard his voice from that evening, strong and confident, a man who had gone beyond romantic dreams whispered under a bed of stars. She longed for a cooling breeze to jolt her out of this muggy mood she had slipped into.

"David was Laura's father," she said.

"Rachel, you know what I mean."

She turned to face her father. His eyes were lost in the shadows and the faint flickering of the lightning did not illuminate them. "You're right, Dad. It doesn't matter anymore. He's long gone from here."

"So?"

"So, there's no point in dragging out old forgotten names. There's nothing to be gained from letting the anger grow again. Laura's my daughter and David was as good a father as she could have hoped for. The past is over."

Rachel wasn't sure she believed that, not with Ben so close again, but that was the way it had to be. For Laura's sake. For her father's sake. There was nothing to be gained from opening Pandora's box at this stage. In a few weeks, she and Laura and her parents would be gone from here, all on to new lives in other places.

"It's getting late," her father said. "I'd best be

going in." There was anger in his voice if not in his actual words as he turned away.

He was almost at the door when she spoke. "Good night, Dad."

"Good night, Rachel. See you in the morning." His voice had softened slightly and he went into the house. The screen door closed quietly after him.

Rachel stayed out in the darkness for only a few minutes more. The distant lightning continued to flash, but she could make no sense of its rhythm. There was just the feeling of impending danger, of power and rage waiting to be unleashed on them. She walked—fled—back inside, where the distractions of television and conversation would ease the tensions building in her heart.

Eleven forty-eight. The digital clock on Rachel's bedside table blinked once. Eleven forty-nine. She sat up in bed. She had already thrown off her covers, but the air felt so stale and stuffy she couldn't get comfortable. It must be getting cooler outside, she thought, for the air-conditioning had automatically turned off.

She got up and walked to the window. The storm gods were closer now and their rumblings were easily heard. Their children had grown larger and bolder, casting rods of lightning ever nearer as they taunted her. She sank into the old Chippendale chair and stared out at the church spire above the library.

It was strange that her mother had assigned her and Laura these rooms lately. As a child Rachel had snuck into this room, hiding here on rainy days to dream of the future. And this was where she'd waited as a sixteen-year-old, pregnant and miserable and trying to find the courage to tell her parents. For hours one Sunday she'd sat up here, staring down at the campus sparkling with Christmas decorations and a gently falling snow. Her parents had been hosting a faculty tea downstairs, and when the last guest had left she'd swallowed her fears and gone downstairs.

Nothing had been the same after that. Her father had always been strict, but they'd had a closeness, a tender bond of love and affection. Her news had shattered that. He'd never forgiven her for not telling him who the father of her child was. They'd never been able to return to that gentle understanding. Why hadn't she told him about Ben? Funny, she couldn't really remember the reasons anymore, just that she had been so alone and so afraid.

Fear wasn't something she'd known with Ben. He had taught her to reach beyond fear, to give love freely, regardless of the cost. Not love of the body at first but love of the heart and soul. Trusting another to love her back. Not being afraid to smile, to laugh, to give of herself. Of course, in giving of herself, she had given her body to him. They had joined in celebration of their love for each other. It had never seemed wrong, never immoral. It had seemed the natural expression of their feelings, regardless of the cost.

And the cost had not been Laura. No, Laura had been a bonus. The cost had been losing Ben. Rachel had gambled that his love for her was strong enough to withstand the secrecy and her need to keep their love from her father. She had gambled and she had lost.

She turned sharply from the window and rubbed her forehead. It was so damn stuffy in the house. Everything seemed to be closing in on her.

Had Ben been bothered by today's meeting? she wondered. But then, why should he be? To him, the past was nothing more than a few brief trysts in the park. He didn't know about Laura.

Rachel's oversize nightshirt was normally cool on the muggiest of summer nights, but tonight it seemed confining and heavy. She sprang up from the chair and flew out of the room as if all her memories were chasing her. If she didn't get some air soon, she would die of suffocation.

She let herself out the front door into the darkness of the night, and was bathed with an immediate sense of relief. Everything was cooler. The wood porch floor felt wonderful to her bare feet and the wind tossed her short curls about, blowing a feeling of renewal into every corner of her body, blowing the memory of Ben's touch from her soul. She took deep, gulping breaths, satisfying the craving of her lungs for the fresh air. Sanity eased back into her mind.

She leaned against a post at the far corner of the porch, relaxed and calm. The air was heavy with moisture. Dad was right, she thought. It was going to rain in a matter of minutes.

A bolt of lightning released an enormous clap of thunder, but Rachel didn't jump back. Instead, her body seemed to reach out to the violent elements. She wanted to be part of them. Hungers had been storming inside her since seeing Ben again. They called out, straining to join the storm of nature.

The wind began throwing huge drops onto her face and body. She didn't move. Rain poured over her, wetting her hair and soaking the front of her nightshirt, but it was wonderfully soothing. The storm within her eased. Ben and her need of him were a part of the past. They would stay there. She could make sure they would.

Suddenly a flash of lightning highlighted a white-shirted figure running up the sidewalk. The darkness swallowed the person up, but she heard footsteps bounding up the stairs and onto the porch. She held her breath.

Another bolt came, lighting the porch and the figure standing near the stairs. It was Ben.

Three

When the lightning flashed again an instant later, Ben walked over to Rachel. His nearness sparked unsettling longings within her, and she turned to look out over the front yard. She'd been wrong in thinking the violent storm had soothed her inner fire. It had instead awakened raging needs. Memories of passion washed over her, confusing the past with the present, dreams with reality. Ben's touch from years ago haunted her, but it was this new Ben, this strong man beside her, that her body was crying out for. She needed time to sort all this out.

"Quite a storm," he said. "The weatherman predicted it was going to miss us."

"Dad said it was going to hit before midnight."

"Oh."

Ben shook his head and swept his wet hair back with his hand. She longed to do that herself. He seemed so close, closer than the few feet that actually separated them. Her heart was racing, and her breath caught in her throat as it always had in the past, yet the pull was stronger now than it ever had been.

"Might as well finish my dash to my apartment," he said.

"Dad said it wasn't going to last long." Why had she said that? she wondered. She was playing with fire, standing here in the darkness with Ben. To be here alone in the night and want him so . . . Was she hoping the past would repeat itself?

"Oh," he said again.

She didn't try to fill the silence. She couldn't speak. It was taking all her willpower to stare out into the night and not at him. He wiped the rain from his face. She saw the movement out of the corner of her eye and ached for those fingers to brush her face that way. She locked her errant gaze on the tightly closed clematis buds. She wasn't a teenager anymore; she would not be caught up in a wave of desire.

"I guess I could stay awhile," he said. His voice was rough, sparking shivers down her spine. "If you don't mind the company."

"No, not at all," she said. She was surprised that her own voice was quiet and almost steady, belying her inner turmoil.

The lightning flashed less frequently as they watched the pouring rain. Rachel's heartbeat slowed to normal, but there was no way she could forget that she and Ben were together, just them and the night. The darkness, the warm gentle breeze of summer, and them. Her heart forgot it was supposed to stay steady, and she searched for something to say, anything that would break the spell around them.

"It was stuffy inside," she said. "I came out for a breath of air."

"Gets that way inside when it cools outside."

"I hadn't expected any guests." Certainly not him.

"I was meeting with a few of the resident counselors and time got away from us. The storm came on so suddenly I got caught."

The rain seemed to be slackening, she noticed. Would he be leaving now? She felt the weight of the storm depress her again. She wanted to be free to think. The cool night air was supposed to have helped her do that, but she didn't want Ben to leave. Not yet.

"Do you visit your folks very often?" he asked.

"Not as often as I'd like to. We've been busy."

"I guess raising a child takes a lot of your time."

He seemed relaxed, as if her presence had no effect on him. Well, then neither would his nearness bother her, she vowed. "Laura really wasn't that much trouble," she said. Her voice was cool and crisp. "But I also helped David with the bookstores. He handled the business end and I selected our stock and handled advertising and marketing."

"Are you running the stores yourself now?"

"No. I decided to sell them after David died since I didn't have the knack for management, but now I'm kind of sorry I did. I miss them." Missed the happy distraction the work provided, she clarified silently.

"Some decisions are like that," Ben said. "Either way, you give up something."

How easily he said that! she thought, remembering her decision to keep Laura. Her parents had been sure she'd give the child up for adoption. They had counseled her on the problems of single mothers, single high school mothers in particular. But she hadn't been able to give up the product of her and Ben's love. Even if he hadn't really cared about her, she had loved him with a true and faithful heart. She could not have lived without Laura, and Ben's easy remark ignited the fury that lay deep in her soul.

What would he know about giving something up? she asked herself angrily. What agony had he ever suffered over one of his decisions? Did he know what it was like to want the best of everything for your child, fully aware that by not giving her up for adoption you had denied her her best chance at happiness? How many nights had he spent sleepless, as she had, cradling her infant daughter even as she was cursing her selfishness at keeping her?

"Laura looks so much like you," he said. "Looking at her is like looking into the past."

Something in his voice—sadness? longing?—made her turn to him. Her bitterness died. She remembered those nights in the park, those precious moments of clinging and loving, of belonging totally to another and believing that that love would go on forever. She remembered the excitement of slipping away from her house under the cover of darkness and racing to meet Ben. Her Ben. She remembered the final argument, the acrid words that had been said, and her stubborn refusal to bend. It was her own fault that she'd suffered such guilt, not his.

But even as her mind wondered what her life would have been like if Ben had taken her home that stormy night fifteen years ago, her gaze was caressing the man before her. His wet shirt had molded itself to his body, showing her that the muscles of his youth had grown more powerful with time. Her body warmed with a hunger that had nothing to do with memories of past summer nights. She wanted him now.

He boldly stared back at her, his gaze traveling over her slender body. He had thought she was beautiful before, but after the birth of a child and so many years, she wondered if he still found her attractive. In the darkness she thought she saw his mouth curve into a sensuous smile, saw his hand begin to lift as if to touch her, caress her.

Whatever fire had burned between them long ago, whatever current of charged desire had pulled them together, the attraction was still just as strong. It hadn't died away with the passage of time. In fact, it seemed even more potent. Her body ached for his touch, her soul cried out for his embrace. But somewhere deep amid the passion, a bit of sanity reigned. Too much had happened in the past fifteen years, too many questions remained unanswered, for her to rush into Ben's arms.

She stepped back, realizing that his shirt wasn't the only one that had molded itself to a body. Her own white T-shirt was clinging to her, and as slowly and inconspicuously as possible she raised her arms and folded them across her chest. She looked at him again and was surprised that even in the shadowy night she could see the raw hunger in his eyes. She turned away. The chasm of unspoken words that lay between them was still waiting to be crossed.

"Laura has her father's eyes," she said, taking the first step across that gulf. But as the words flew through the air, she held her breath. What was she doing? Did she really mean to tell Ben about Laura now? She had written to tell him years ago, but he hadn't answered her letter. Had he read it? Or hadn't he even gotten it?

"David was a very lucky man," he said.

His voice dragged her gaze back to him. He didn't know. Whatever had happened to that letter, he hadn't read it.

"David's left a part of himself behind," Ben went on, his voice unsteady, as it were an effort for him to speak so casually. "In the long run, that's all that really counts in this world."

She bit her lip, a mélange of feelings swirling around inside her. Was now the time to tell Ben that Laura was his daughter? He was in a sensitive position. A college president wasn't supposed to have children from past affairs turning up. The truth about Laura could cost him his job. A safer route appeared and she dove for it.

"Is that what you're doing with the college?" she asked. "Leaving a part of yourself behind?"

"I'm hoping to," he said. "Your father's built a marvelous institution here, but it needs a more vigorous marketing plan now, and that's where I come in. Without your father's efforts though, I wouldn't have anything to sell."

She laughed. "You make it sound like toothpaste or used cars."

He shrugged. "Some people look down on marketing. But a lot of small colleges are going to die, and that's a tragedy. The student base is decreasing and we can't just wait for them to find us."

"I didn't mean to—"

"Small colleges have made unique contributions throughout the history of our country," he went on. "We can't let them die. We have to fight for them. Otherwise, the work of people like your father will die and all of us and our future generations will be the worse for it."

Somehow the rain had washed away Ben's veneer of sophistication and Rachel saw the idealistic young man he'd been fifteen years before. His eyes were bright with care and concern. His hair was hanging down over his forehead just as it had when he was eighteen.

The fires rose within her again, and she wanted to reach out and hold him tight. She wanted to give him all her love, both physically and emotionally. She wanted to support him, to encourage him. The world needed people like Ben Healey. Needed them to hold back the darkness of ignorance and apathy, and she could help him. She could soothe him and recharge his energies so that, strong and confident, he could ride forth against the dragons. But even as he took a step closer to her, as if the fires were calling to him also, she stepped backward. Things were moving too fast. The past had taught her caution if nothing else.

"It's stopped raining," she said.

"What?" he asked in confusion and surprise.

"The rain." She pointed. "It stopped."

He looked out into the darkness. "So it has."

She wanted him to go; she wanted him to stay. Torn by her yearnings, she watched the drops run slowly off the clematis vine that was entangled around a side post. "Funny how August rains never seem to cool anything off," she said.

"There's a chill in the air from this one," he said. "You'd better go in before you catch cold."

She turned to him. His eyes were shadowed, yet still fiery with desire. An answering blaze coursed through her. How could she ever be cold when her skin was burning with the fever of passion? But to stay out here was to flirt with danger. Too often in the past she had let her desires choose her path. She had grown. It was time to think, if thought was still possible.

"Yes, I'll go in now," she said. Was it rationality or fear that was speaking?

The storm clouds were blowing past and the moon dimly illuminated the two of them. Their bodies seemed to seek each other, called by memories of nights long past. Ben moved closer as a powerful force pulled at them, attempting to make them one. Only inches separated them. Inches and years. Rachel knew she had to be strong tonight.

"Good night, Ben."

He hesitated. "Good night, Rachel."

The words were mere breaths on the night air. All she had to do was lean forward ever so slightly and she'd be in his arms, but some nameless worry held her back.

"Go inside," he said. He touched her shoulder gently, with hidden restraint, and strode quickly down the stairs.

Rachel was left standing, left yearning. She shivered slightly. She hadn't thought it possible, but here she was getting chilled.

"Aren't you feeling well this morning, dear? You seem so quiet. Is it too warm up here for you?"

Rachel looked across the dusty attic at her mother. "I'm fine. It's fine." The large fan they'd brought up with them was circulating the pleasantly cool air left over from last night's rain. It was actually one of the better days to rummage through the attic, picking what would be saved and what would be discarded.

"I just didn't sleep that well last night," Rachel explained, and went back to poking through an old dresser. She pulled open a drawer filled with outgrown clothes. There were blouses and sweaters, even some old cotton slips she'd worn when she was about fifteen. "Want these with the clothes you're giving away?" she asked.

Her mother walked over to look through them. "Do you think they'd fit Laura?" she asked, holding up a short-sleeved blouse trimmed in ecru lace. "Oh, dear, there's a stain on this." She picked at the stain with her fingernail. "I wonder what it is."

"Chocolate ice cream."

Jessica stared at her. "Fancy you remembering that after all these years."

Not really, Rachel thought. She had been wearing that blouse at a faculty picnic, wishing she were elsewhere, when a tall, outrageously dressed young man with the most beautiful eyes in the world had bumped into her, causing her to spill ice cream on herself.

"I don't suppose it'll come out after all this time," Jessica said.

Rachel started, then realized her mother was still rubbing the stain. "I doubt it. Besides, my daughter's allergic to any clothes that aren't permanent press."

Jessica laughed and picked up a handful of the clothes. "How true! I'd forgotten just how much has changed since you were Laura's age."

And how much hadn't, Rachel mused. Last night's midnight meeting with Ben still ached in her heart. A sultry August night and Ben were a mighty powerful combination. She dragged her mind, kicking and screaming, back to the task at hand and cleaned out the rest of the drawer. The pile of old clothes in the middle of the floor was growing. Her hungers did not have to follow suit, she told herself.

"What about these boxes of papers?" she asked, pointing to a pile in the corner.

The past was past and it would stay there, she continued silently. While she couldn't stop the memories from tickling at her, she did not have to acknowledge them. She didn't have to let the desire in her grow. She had a good life now and was doing quite well, even though there was an emptiness with David gone, an emptiness that a tiger was trying to push its way into.

"Rachel," her mother said. "Are you sure you're feeling well?"

"I'm fine." This time she didn't bother trying to hide her impatience. "Now, what do you want done with these boxes?"

"I told you they were college papers. Your father's leaving them to the history department for their archives."

"Oh." Rachel took a deep breath and chased through the corners of her mind. No tigers, no lions, no bears. Everybody out. "All right. Then what do we work on next?"

"Next, we'll go downstairs and have some lemonade."

"Mother. I told you I'm fine. Now, let's get to work."

But Jessica resolutely turned off the fan and led the way down to the kitchen. While her mother made a pitcher of lemonade, Rachel stared out the window at her mother's vegetable garden. Two small rabbits were nibbling at the lettuce. Should she tell her mother now or wait until the rabbits had eaten their fill?

"Did you remember Dr. Healey from the summer he stayed here with his uncle?" Jessica asked as she put a glass of lemonade in front of Rachel.

Rachel turned. Her mother's face swam before her eyes. Dr. Healey? There had been a boy named Ben that summer. A tall, slender boy with black hair and compelling eyes, eyes that could reach down deep and capture her soul.

"Sort of," Rachel answered, and stared at her glass.

"Of course he was just a boy then," her mother said. "He's a man now."

Yes, he is. Strong and virile and filled with burning desires. Any woman would feel his attraction; the only reason Rachel felt it more strongly was because the past made her vulnerable. Once she got over the shock of seeing Ben again, she'd be able to control her wayward thoughts and her wayward body. She looked up to find her mother gazing at her.

"Yes," she said lamely. "I guess he has changed some in all those years."

She escaped her mother's scrutiny by looking back at the garden. The rabbits were still there. They were filling up today. She should tell her mother, but she wouldn't. She knew what it was like to crave something forbidden, to be allowed only a brief taste of paradise.

"He ought to marry," Jessica said.

"Who?"

Jessica laughed. "Dr. Healey. Who else were we talking about?"

"Oh, yes."

"Are you sure you're feeling all right?" Jessica asked. "Your body's here, but your mind seems far, far away."

Instead of replying, Rachel took a long drink of lemonade. She set the glass back down precisely in the ring of condensation it had left on the vinyl tabletop. Her mother's question nagged at her. "Why do you think he should be married?" she asked.

"The president's position really requires two people," Jessica said. "There's so much entertaining and speaking to different groups that a single man can't do it all."

"Then they should hire two people," Rachel said. Her gaze drifted to the garden again, but the rabbits were gone. There was no distraction from the thoughts that tormented her. Did Ben have a fiancée? Did he even have a lady friend, a lover? Fear burned in her stomach and she grew annoyed at herself. She didn't care if Ben was engaged.

"A man like Dr. Healey really ought to be married," Jessica said.

So much for brave talk, Rachel thought. Hearing her mother say the words destroyed the fragile wall she had built around her heart. She didn't want Ben to care for another woman, to laugh with someone else, to love another, to be there when this other woman needed him. She swallowed hard to force the pain away.

"Mother, I understand the duties of a college president quite well, but I don't have control over Dr. Healey's marital status. You don't have to convince me."

"I wasn't just talking about his duties," her mother said. "He looks like a family man."

"Family man?"

"Yes. He looks like a natural father. He needs children to love."

That pain grew until it was raw, agonizing. Ben had a child to love. A wonderful little girl. Rachel took a deep breath and forced back the tears that wanted to flow.

"You're right," she said brightly to her mother as she got to her feet. "I am rather in a fog this morning. If you can spare me, I think I'll take a walk. Maybe it'll wake me up."

"Go ahead, dear," Jessica said, but Rachel was already fleeing out the back door. The air was cool and soothing, but the pain was still there.

For the next hour or so, Rachel wandered around

the almost deserted campus, letting the warm rays of the sun melt the tension from her shoulders. She finally arrived at the student union and sat down on the edge of the fountain in front of it. She took her shoes off and idly splashed her feet in the water, ignoring the shocked little voice inside her. She didn't care if the pool was off limits; she wasn't a student here. Ripples raced across the surface of the water to fade at the far edges of the pool, and a sigh escaped from her.

What was she going to do about Ben and Laura? she wondered. Did Ben have a right to know that Laura was his daughter? Of course he did. Rachel had no hesitation about admitting that. But how, and when, should she tell him? How would she tell Laura?

There was no question in Rachel's mind that the telling would have to be done. Laura's parentage wasn't something Ben would stumble on accidentally. Even if Laura wore her glasses and everyone saw the true color of her eyes, Rachel doubted anyone would compare them to Ben's eyes. No, she was going to have to find the right time and place for the truth.

"Oh, Lord," she said aloud. "I wish I had stayed back home where life was simple!" She pulled her feet from the water and rested them on the warm concrete for the air to dry them.

Calm had just begun to fill her again when a shadow fell across her. "Hello there," a man said.

Four

Rachel didn't have to look. She knew it was Ben. Even if she hadn't heard his voice, her body would have known it was he. She tilted her head back slowly to gaze up at him.

"Out for a walk?" he asked.

She tried to cool her sensual awareness of him with humor and nodded toward the fountain. "I was thinking of a swim actually."

He laughed and sat down beside her—too close for any possible coherency of thought. "That's pretty brave talk for someone familiar with this school and all its rules," he said.

"Why? They can't give me a detention or a suspension." She eyed the three marble figures in the center of the fountain with annoyance, as if they were the root of her worries. "You know, if those women are really pouring truth, honor, and knowledge into the pool, wading in the water seems the best way to absorb it."

"So that's the story they told you?" Ben looked at her sadly, then shook his head. "Must have thought you were too impressionable to be told the truth."

"Oh, and what is the truth?"

He gazed at the figures. "Those aren't truth, honor, and knowledge. They're beauty, passion, and desire. If you wade in the waters from their urns, you'll fall in love with whoever's in the pool with you."

"Be it fish or fowl?" She laughed, and he looked at her questioningly. "They used to have goldfish in the pool. Can you imagine what kind of romances sprang up?"

"All right, Miss Know-It-All," he said. "Want to go wading with me?"

The challenge in his eyes and the dare in his voice reminded her of last night, of the longings she'd lain alone with long after the storm inside her and outside her had passed. She remembered the hurt and fear she'd fought against this morning when her mother had suggested that Ben should marry. Why did she have to meet him today? He was the last person she needed to see. So why had she chosen to walk through the campus? she asked herself. Why hadn't she gone to the downtown shopping area or to the docks along the river if she wanted to avoid Ben?

"Actually," he said, as if he'd read her thoughts, "you're just the person I was hoping to come across."

"Oh?" She appreciated the reprieve from his challenge, but her body was warming in its own interpretation of his innocent words.

"I'm having trouble laying out my office and need some advice."

"I'm not sure I'm particularly qualified," she said. She moved her feet and watched the sun dry the damp print left on the concrete.

"Sure, you are," he said. "I want the place to look warm and welcoming, and that's always been your specialty."

What did that mean? she wondered. But she was afraid to ask and stayed silent.

"I was just going over to the house now," he said. "Maybe we could arrange a time to meet there."

"Why not now?" She'd been telling herself she could withstand his nearness, that she was an adult and not susceptible to inner swoonings. Now was the time to prove it to herself. She got to her feet, picking up her moccasins.

"Are you sure you have time?" he asked.

"Positive."

She began to walk, swinging her moccasins boldly in her hand, and Ben joined her. They strolled through the shade of the rustling oak trees and through the sunny stretches where the sidewalk was hot from the sun. There was no one else in sight and Ben's closeness, his height and powerful build, seemed all the more intimidating. Rachel's mouth grew dry as they passed Science Hall. The silence seemed deafening and she fought for something to say.

"How did you happen to be chosen as president here?" she asked.

"Doubting my qualifications?" His voice was light and amused. No hungers seemed to be taunting him, stealing his breath and his sanity. The desire she had sensed in him the night before must have been a momentary weakness on his part.

"Just curious," she said. "You must admit, it's quite a coincidence."

"Maybe not."

They passed the tennis courts. A teenage couple was playing, laughing and missing more balls than they hit. Were her yearnings for Ben as obvious as the teenagers' love? Rachel wondered.

"I've always liked it here," he said, "and when I heard that they were looking for someone to take your father's place, I made a few calls."

"That's all it took?"

"That's all it took to get interviewed." He smiled at her, a warm, teasing smile. "My charm did the rest."

"I see." She tried to smile as lightly, with the same carefree abandon, but she couldn't. No matter how she tried, she couldn't keep her awareness of him at bay.

She was glad when they reached the house. Inside, he opened the door to his office, then stepped aside for her to enter. She had seen the room yesterday, of course, and knew that the furniture was the same as her father had had. But the room no longer bore her father's personality. Did everything Ben touch change? she wondered. Did he have the Midas touch, only rather than gold, he put a glow on things, an aura of warmth? He walked across the room while she stayed near the door, still holding her shoes.

"The room is a good size," he said, "and the furniture is fine. But it just isn't me. I can't say what's wrong exactly though."

She could. Or thought she could. But was the Ben she knew the real Ben, or an imagined one?

"The room is like my father," she said. It wasn't easy to ignore the flutterings in her stomach when Ben's eyes held hers. "I can still see him sitting here, gold-rimmed glasses, dark suit, and starched white collar. Authority flowing out of every pore. Everyone—faculty, students, and me—approached that desk timidly, hat in hand. I don't ever remember seeing a smile in here."

Ben looked sad, and walked over to her. "You sound like you did when you were a teenager. Surely, your father must have gotten less strict as you got older."

She gazed up at him, only a few steps away from her. His eyes were tender, his voice gentle. She wished she were in his arms, that she could let him make her confusion disappear. But more than just these few steps separated them. Was now the time to tell him the truth, that more than memories lingered from that summer?

But there were other memories besides the good ones with Ben, and her father's office was not the place to reveal secrets long hidden.

"What I'd do," she said, turning away from him, from her own longings, "is split the office into work areas. I'd make one section into a private work area and then another part could be a relaxed sitting area, where you could meet with students, faculty, trustees. That kind of thing."

Ben nodded. Whatever solace his eyes had been offering was gone. He was the college president now, the leader, the man in control. His gaze was taking in the room, not her. The thoughtful look on his face was for her ideas, not for her.

"That sounds good," he said.

Braver now that she felt more in control of herself, Rachel walked over to the windows behind the desk. The deep pile rug was soft against her feet, adding to the muddle of sensations tugging at her. She set her shoes on top of a stack of magazines on the windowsill and turned. As she studied the room, she was careful not to look at Ben.

Her gaze lingered on the small alcove behind the door. "Why not put your desk over there?" she asked.

Ben looked at the area consideringly.

"Then," she continued, "you could put those two sofas over here by the window for a sitting area."

He nodded.

"And where the sofas are now, you could put in a small round table for a conference area."

"Doesn't sound half bad," he said. "Do you think the desk will fit back there?"

"Half bad?" she repeated, pretending affront. But his mocking tone at least had broken the spell. They had been friends first, before they'd been lovers. Maybe they could be friends again.

"Do you think the desk will fit?" he repeated.

"If those are real muscles under that shirt, we can move it and see."

His eyes laughed at her. "That old desk is heavy."

"We can take the drawers out."

He stared at her for a moment, then started pulling drawers out and stacking them. She did the same on the other side, then they half-carried, half-dragged the desk to the alcove. Rachel could feel his laughter, but she refused to grunt or groan.

After they wrestled the desk into place, Ben stood back to survey the scene. "Looks good," he said, and pointed to a shelf behind the desk. "I can put my personal computer back there. There's a power outlet underneath."

"I know," she teased. "I thought of all that. So quit your stalling and grab the end of that sofa."

The time passed quickly as they pushed the rest of the furniture around. They tried the sofas several ways, but finally arranged them the way Rachel had suggested in the beginning. When they were through, they fell onto one, tired and laughing.

"And I thought the life of a college president was going to be cerebral," Ben said wryly as he stretched his arms over his head. "Why did I bother with all that schooling to be a furniture mover?"

"You aren't exactly done," Rachel said. "You still need a table for that conference area and a lowboy to put between these sofas."

"Sounds good to me," he said, and lay against the back of the sofa, closing his eyes. "Let me know when you've got them in place."

"Let you know! It's your job to move the furniture around, not mine. Why else do you think they hired somebody so young for this job?"

He opened his eyes. They were dancing with laughter. "Not my charm, huh?"

It felt good to laugh with him again. "What charm? With it and a quarter, you might be able to buy yourself a cup of coffee."

"Oh, is that so?"

Suddenly, their gazes locked together and the laughter died. There had been a time when his charm had been powerful indeed, when his whispered words could set her heart aflame as her body hungered for his touch. And not just long ago either. Last night they had both felt the power of their needs, of the hidden desire that seemed to flare to life at a look from the other.

"Ben," she whispered, a prayer on the wind, an aching of her soul.

He reached for her and suddenly she was in his arms. His lips came home to hers, and it was as if they'd never been apart. Longing leaped into a blazing fire, engulfing her breath, her sanity. She was sixteen again and wild with love. His hands moved slowly over her back, bringing her closer. But he wasn't eighteen anymore. A man's body was pressed against hers; a man's solid strength was surrounding her.

Her hands were on his chest, then his shoulders, then her arms wound around his neck as his mouth urged hers to open, as his kiss deepened into a song of memories. This wasn't the past though. The past had never been this fiery, this all-consuming, or this natural. His lips finally left hers and she rested her head against his chest, her eyes closed. His arms enclosed her, cutting off the worries, the realities of the world. She was safe; she was home.

But just as abruptly as the fires had flared and threatened to consume her, sanity returned. Slowly she pulled away. Her eyes met Ben's for the briefest of seconds, then their gazes flew apart.

They sat in silence, staring out the window at the library in the distance, at the worn spot in the green carpet, the narrow satin stripes of the sofa.

They looked at everything but each other. The rhythmic ticking of the grandfather clock in the hallway was the only sound, and it seemed to push the tension ever higher, ever tauter.

"Who'd have thought we'd meet like this?" Ben whispered.

Rachel's mouth went dry. Desperately she searched her mind for a bright, witty comment. All she found was blankness.

"I knew when I took the job," he went on, "that there was a good chance I'd see you again." The quietness of his voice dragged her gaze back to him. His eyes were piercing. "I wasn't sure I wanted to."

The gentle laughter in his voice did not ease the solid sinking of her stomach, a feeling equivalent to an elevator plummeting to the basement. "Thanks a lot," she muttered.

He leaned forward, his arms on his knees. "Sometimes dreams have a way of erasing reality, and that summer was so special I didn't want to find out it had been perfect only in my mind."

The elevator stopped and she found a smile to give Ben. "You mean, if I had grown gray and fat?"

He shook his head. "We may all do that eventually. I didn't want to find out that the girl I loved had really been cold or selfish or hard."

His seriousness frightened and tantalized her. She had the sensation that she was standing on the edge of a precipice and Ben was calling to her, begging her to fly across to him. Her natural cautious nature pulled her back into light humor.

"And how would you know now," she asked,

"what I'd been like back then? It was quite a few years ago. We've all changed."

"Not that much."

She stood up and walked to the window. His nearness made her too aware of a silent aching, of an emptiness that she longed to fill. Temptation was easier to fight at a distance. "We both have changed," she said. "We've both grown up."

"Growing up isn't necessarily changing."

But for her it had been. Her safe, protected world had given way to frightening reality. She *had* changed in the past fifteen years. She stared out the window at the world she'd known so long ago. What if she'd reached Ben when she'd learned she was pregnant? What if he'd written to her?

"Did you ever wish things had been different?" she asked, startling herself that she had spoken the words aloud.

"Constantly."

His brusque frankness stunned her, and she spun around to find him right behind her. He was close enough to touch, to hold and love, yet his eyes seemed far away. "I'm always wishing something else had happened," he said. "Especially when I'm struggling with an unforeseen complication."

Was that how he would have seen Laura?

"Don't we all wish we could direct events around us?" he added.

She turned away from him and sat on the edge of the window seat. His presence was still disconcerting, and her heart was racing at the promise of passion in his voice. But she would not be distracted. "I meant us," she explained. "I was thinking of the way we parted. Did you ever wish we hadn't fought?"

Even as the words echoed in the air, she wondered why she was asking them. Was she seeking to be hurt? Her gaze crept back to him. He was perched on the arm of a chair, studying his hands as if wisdom were hidden there.

"Things happen for a reason," he said slowly. "We were pretty heavily involved for kids so young. I think we both had a lot of maturing to do. Maturing we had to do alone."

She hadn't been alone, she thought. She'd been with Laura. Her mother's cousin had provided her and Laura with a home for a time. Indirectly, Mary had also provided a husband, when she had introduced Rachel to her neighbor, David Anders, a quiet man almost twenty years older than Rachel and widowed soon after Laura had been born. David had been someone to lean on, someone who like being needed, and who filled that ache in Rachel to be held and taken care of. But she remembered now that it had been those first years, those hard years of self-doubt, the painful, guilt-ridden nights, when she had grown up.

The past suddenly seemed like a huge gulf, too wide and too deep even to think of jumping over. She retraced her steps back to the sofa.

"I expected you to write," she said quietly. "You didn't."

He looked up at her. His smile was sad. "It wasn't that I didn't want to, I just thought it best that I didn't."

Best? What did that mean? But she couldn't force the question out. She wanted to ask him if he'd gotten her letter and ignored it, but the gulf was wide enough already. If he said yes, the distance would become uncrossable.

A knock on the door offered Rachel a chance to breathe. She turned and saw Laura standing in the doorway, her gaze stern as it went from Ben to Rachel.

"Grandma said to tell you that lunch is ready," Laura said, her voice almost angry. Was she picking up her grandfather's possessiveness about the college and the presidency? Rachel wondered.

"Thank you, honey," she said. Her daughter left and took the tension with her, but the intimacy between her and Ben did not return. An embarrassed awkwardness filled the void.

Ben cleared his throat. "I'd better get going. I promised the head of the English department that I'd meet with him around lunchtime."

Rachel got to her feet as he did.

"Thanks for all your help," he said briskly.

"That's okay," she said, shrugging. "Let me know if you want to move any more furniture around."

There was no return to their lighthearted humor, though, just as there was no return to the passion. With a quick smile he left, and she stared out the window to see a flicker of his shadow as he passed. Love you, bear your child, move your furniture. She shook her head to will back the mistiness in her eyes and went to lunch.

Five

Ten thousand fierce Peshtigo warriors were massed outside the princess's castle for a final assault. Over three hundred soldiers lay dead on the castle grounds, and now the captain of the princess's own personal guard lay dying, an arrow through his throat and a long curved sword in his stomach. The hero, a wandering minstrel who was really the prince of a kingdom in the far misty mountains, lay on a remote forest trail, his leg pinned beneath his dead horse.

Rachel yawned and laid the thick paperback aside. It was so comfortable and peaceful here in her parents' backyard gazebo that she had trouble getting greatly concerned about the princess's problems. She yawned again as she stretched her arms high overhead, then lay back on the lounge chair. She had forgotten how beautiful it was here. There was nothing like the old gazebo on a sultry August morning.

Five days had passed since she and Laura had arrived. Five days of cleaning out attics, closets, and cabinets. Five days of alternately avoiding Ben and hoping to see him. She was glad to have the day off while her mother went to a final garden club meeting.

Rachel's eyelids lowered as she stared at the heat waves shimmering above the green lawn. A dragonfly zipped about over the vegetable garden. What was Ben doing today? she wondered. Did he spend hours dreaming of her as she spent dreaming of him? She let her eyes close all the way and saw again his laughing gaze, his gentle smile, those tender hands.

A mosquito buzzed near her ear and she waved it away. Funny, she thought. Here she was lying in the gazebo and daydreaming just as she had as a child. Every summer, for as long as she had lived here, this little white castle in the backyard had been hers to escape to, along with her story-book heroes and princesses.

Every summer, that is, until the last one. Then she'd had her own prince in Ben. That summer she would run out here and dream of the future instead of the past, an immediate future that didn't extend beyond the coming evening. A future as passionate and full of love as any of her books.

Now it was summer again, and Ben had captured her thoughts again. Not much had changed.

"Hi."

Rachel sprang upright, a startled cry escaping her lips.

"I'm sorry," Ben said as he stepped up into the gazebo. "I tried to give you fair warning."

She eased back against the lounger, willing her heart back to a normal speed. She took a slow, deep breath. Her heart wasn't racing only because she'd been startled. "That's okay," she said. "I was just daydreaming."

"It's a good day for it."

He sat down next to her, and his hand brushed—accidentally?—against her bare leg. A shiver ran through her, and she commanded her body to stay in line. Ben was smiling at her, his eyes bright and intense, as if he knew the havoc his nearness was creating in her. She avoided his gaze and looked out over the lawn.

"How's your book?" he asked.

She turned to see him staring down at the cover, at the hero, sword held high, an expanse of his magnificent bronzed chest bared.

"Okay," she said.

"Is the hero exciting?" Ben's blue-green eyes sparkled at her.

She looked down at the hero again. His brown eyes stared flatly. "No," she answered. "Actually he's rather ordinary." But who wouldn't be when compared to Ben?

Her heart rate was still high, but she congratulated herself on her calm exterior. She took another deep breath and dared her own question. "How are your heroines?"

"Exceptionally ordinary."

A slight smile curved her lips as she wrapped the ensuing silence comfortably around her soulders. Exceptionally ordinary. Why should that please her so?

"How is your father coming along?" he asked.

"He seems to be progressing very nicely."

"I've seen him taking walks with Laura. He looks good."

"Yes, having Laura around seems to be the best medicine for him." Her father had looked happier and more at ease in the last few days than Rachel could ever remember.

"She's a fine young lady," Ben said.

"Yes," Rachel said with a small laugh. "Usually."

"You must be very proud of her."

"Usually." This time she only smiled.

"Her father was a fortunate man," Ben went on. "It's too bad that he won't see her grow into a woman."

Rachel stared straight ahead, not daring to look into those tiger eyes. Laura's father could see her grow into a woman if he wanted. If she found the strength to tell him. She blinked back her fears and stole a quick glance at Ben out of the corner of her eye. He was staring straight ahead also, his gaze fixed on the apple tree at the far end of the yard. His jaw was clenched and a vein was pulsing fiercely in his temple. Why was he upset? she wondered. Was it the thought of her having been married to another man? She wanted to tell him about Laura, but told herself, again, that it wasn't the right time. There was still too much tension between them.

"How is the new president getting along?" she asked gently.

Slowly the strain ebbed from his body. She could see the throbbing vein quiet and the jaw unclench. When he had relaxed himself, he turned to her.

"He's trying," he said, "but isn't getting much

cooperation. The board of trustees was all in favor of hiring me last month, but now that your father's recovering faster than they expected, half of them think they were too hasty."

"The politics of a small college are just as rough as any of the state capitals," she said.

"It's not just that. There's so much misunderstanding and hurt. I don't want to push your father out of the position if he still wants it, but I would really like the chance to help this school grow too. So many people have worked hard and they've built an outstanding college. A really beautiful place, where students are intellectually challenged and spiritually nurtured."

As had happened that stormy night a few days earlier, the hardening of the years faded from his face and the soft features of a boy—an earnest, caring boy concerned with justice and opportunity for all—took their place. Rachel remembered impassioned speeches on the bluffs, the moonlight sneaking through the branches to light up those tiger eyes, making them seem like twin fireflies. Love surrounded her. Tenderness, fear, desire, and the promise of unbounded happiness rose within her, and she had to turn away. She needed the peaceful solitude of the garden to help her breathe again.

"We have to tell people about this place," Ben continued. "We have to get out to the high schools, the junior highs even. We have to go to the media. We have to tell everyone what a great school we have. Not enough people know about it, and in today's era of declining enrollments, we can die.

And I think the world would be poorer for it if that happened."

Ben hadn't changed at all, she thought, smiling. The voice was a little deeper, the beard a little darker, but he was still her Ben.

"I really need to talk to your father," he said.

"He's right there," she said, nodding toward the house. "Why don't you just march in and demand that he talk to you?"

Ben laughed a little, rubbing his face and eyes with both hands. "It's not that easy. He refuses to see me. Even if I confronted him face to face, he still could refuse to talk to me. He certainly won't give me the help I need until he chooses to."

She stared at him, seeing the strain of weariness around his mouth. With all the other worries and concerns rushing around her, she had been ignoring most of the talk about the changeover, but now she saw how deep the trouble was. Things came flooding back. Cryptic comments from Laura, sarcastic remarks from her father, conversation around the school. There was a battle going on. The old versus the new. If the battle continued, both would lose. Even more important, the school would lose.

"I can try to talk to him," she said softly.

The lines of weariness were around Ben's eyes, too, and she looked away, wanting more than anything to ease that tension from him. She wanted to take him in her arms and bring him peace. Fire and raging passion, and then peace.

"Let's take a ride into Galena," he said abruptly.

She turned to look into those tiger eyes and felt herself become lost in his smile. "Sure," she said.

• • •

Ben normally loved the road to Galena, a small, attractive Illinois town not far from Dubuque. Each curve, each hill, was a new beginning. Who knew what vistas lay just ahead, waiting to unfold before him? But today his only enthusiasm came from having Rachel at his side. As for the excitement of discovery, he felt as he had for so much of his high school years—adrift with no real place to which he belonged—no one really to belong to.

The board at the college had hired him, but what did that mean? That a month ago, nine out of the sixteen trustees had been willing to give him a chance. Now that Dr. Dupres was recovering faster and more completely than anyone had expected, some of those nine trustees were shuffling their feet. Why did Ben talk so much about publicity and marketing? they asked. Dr. Dupres had never done that. Why hadn't Ben settled the teachers' contracts? Why hadn't he met with the alumni board? Dr. Dupres always had these things settled by the end of July. Maybe if they all, Dr. Dupres included, would be a bit more cooperative, Ben thought, he would get something accomplished too.

He looked over at Rachel. Funny that they should meet again now. She had been the only stable thing in his life years ago, when his home had been the boarding school and his summers had been visits to one well-meaning relative after another. When the only emotion he'd felt was anger at his parents for dying and leaving him alone.

Then Rachel had come along. Her blue eyes had taken him in, just as her soft smile had soothed his hurts, made them disappear. She still held that same power over him and suddenly he needed to see her smile, needed to pretend, just for a few hours, that they belonged together.

"I'm glad the glaciers left this corner of Illinois alone," he said with a quick smile. "I like these roller-coaster roads."

She returned his smile, but shook her head in mock disgust. "Why are you giving glaciers all the credit?" she asked. "Glaciers had nothing to do with it."

"Oh, no?"

"Obviously you have no Kickapoo blood in you or you'd know the real reason."

"Kickapoo?"

"Don't tease. You know they're the Indian tribe that roamed this area long before the white man broke it up into artificial little chunks named Illinois, Wisconsin, and Iowa."

"Sorry."

They went plunging down a steep, curving hill. Deep valleys ran off either side. Her teasing voice made him see sunshine up ahead, made him feel the sunshine in his blood.

"Long, long ago," she began, "even before the time of man, from the house of the early morning came a giant, hairy beast that was the father of all the buffalo that roam the world today. Herds of this enormous creature followed the sun, stripping the forests in their path and stomping the earth flat."

"And that's how the great plains were made?" Ben asked. "I hope you aren't planning this for your doctoral dissertation topic."

Her glance ordered silence, though her lips were twitching with suppressed laughter. He wanted nothing more than to feel those lips beneath his and flung his gaze back to the road. How could she still have such power over him? Had the long intervening years really existed, or had they been only a dream?

Rachel went on. "The forest animals, led by the bravest of the stags, fought fiercely, but the buffalo were too powerful for them. The stags retreated here and chose a spokesman from among them. A young buck named Hatay, which means 'future chief,' was picked to take their appeal to the Great Spirit."

A straightaway opened up and Ben passed a slow-moving minivan full of sightseers. Rachel's voice had eased the knot of tension from the back of his neck. He felt more relaxed and happier than he'd been in ages.

"Hatay went to the Great Spirit," she continued, "and pleaded the case of the forest people. If all the forests, hills, and valleys were destroyed, the forest animals would disappear from the earth and variety would be lost. The Great Spirit promised to save the forest creatures, but only if they would make a sacrifice. Their bravest stag would have to leave Mother Earth and spend Forever in the house of the Great Spirit."

She paused and Ben glanced over at her. She was looking straight ahead, and the fine, gentle curve of her chin, the firmness of her lips started a smoldering fire within him.

She continued after a moment. "Hatay saw that he had little choice, and said good-bye to Laughing Water, a beautiful doe he had been promised to. Then he went to the house of the Great Spirit while Laughing Water returned to Earth with a heavy heart. And that's why today's deer are such shy creatures. Hatay never fathered any children and his fighting spirit stayed with him in the house of the Great Spirit."

"And Laughing Water?" Ben asked. "What happened to her?"

"She never married and lived a lonely life deep in the forest."

"That's certainly an upbeat ending," he said jokingly, but his thoughts were suddenly bleak. Was there a meaning in this story for him? Was she trying to tell him that she would mourn David's death forever? "Is there a moral to the story, or did you tell it just to set a cheery tone for our day?"

She laughed, and the face she turned toward him wasn't one of sadness, hidden or otherwise. "There's always a million morals to those old stories. What do you need to learn?"

"How about not to bring you along when I need a few laughs?" But he was laughing as he said it.

"That's a great attitude." She pretended to pout. "See if I ever go out with you again."

The silence that eased over them was comfortable. It was like an old warm robe, familiar and relaxing. Ben's desire to get to know Rachel again grew, and so did his courage.

"How did you meet David?" he asked, glancing at her. He needed to look at her as he asked the question. He wanted to know it was all right to talk about David. "You don't have to answer if you don't want to."

"No, I don't mind." Her voice was gentle as always and gave him no clue to her feelings. "He lived near my aunt and I met him while I was visiting her."

"Oh." Her answer was disappointingly ordinary, and Ben felt foolish for wanting to know more. "I thought maybe you'd met him in school, or at the college."

"No."

What more could he ask without appearing to pry? Besides, he wasn't certain what exactly he wanted to know. In spite of the sun and the warm breeze, the day was starting to grow dark and he sought to push back the gloom.

"So tell me about Laura," he said.

"Laura?"

"You know, your daughter." He glanced at Rachel, puzzled by her confusion. She was staring straight ahead. "You're the only mother I know who hasn't talked my ear off about her child."

"We haven't really talked all that much," she said slowly.

"So here's your chance." He smiled at her. "I know where she got her good looks, but tell me if she's as stubborn as you used to be."

"I was never stubborn!" she protested, but it was a weak cry that died in laughter at his skeptical look. "All right, so I was a few times, but not that much."

"How about never taking me home to your father?"

Her laughter faded. "He would have ordered you

off the face of the earth if he'd known about us," she said. "You know how protective he was."

"Actually I don't. I met him only a few times in passing around the college." The hurt he'd felt back when she wouldn't take him home still rankled, but he pushed it aside. He was older now, and had grown used to the feeling of being alone, of watching a family's closeness while ignoring the aching emptiness in his own life.

"Do you suppose he knew all along and that's why he won't see me now?" he asked.

"No!" she said quite firmly. "Believe me, if my father had known about you, I would have heard. He's just hurting now at having to leave the college. He would feel bitter toward anyone who was taking his place."

"I guess."

They entered Galena then, and parked the car. Under the smiling August sun they walked aimlessly among the old buildings and along the red brick sidewalks. Before long, the seriousness of the ride down was forgotten and they were laughing and talking like old friends. The charm of the town wove a spell around them, and soon they were holding hands and whispering silly little jokes like old lovers. The day had turned sweet and Ben was determined to savor every second of it.

"Oh, look!" Rachel exclaimed as they passed the window of an antique shop. "That table would be just right for the conference area in your office."

"Yeah, I suppose so." He couldn't care less about mundane things like furniture and the college. This was his and Rachel's day. Nothing was going to intrude on it.

"Let's go in and look at it."

"Some other time."

"What other time? We're here, and I want to go shopping." She pulled him along toward the door. "Women love to go shopping."

"Why didn't you warn me ahead of time?" he asked, laughing.

"A man your age shouldn't need warnings."

"I spent ten years in this monastery high in the mountains of Tibet," he said. "We lived alone in cells, carved deep in the mountainside. Once a month a holy man would visit us and we would discuss whatever truth we had discovered that month. Then every six months—"

"Come on," she said, scowling fiercely. "We're going shopping and then we'll have lunch."

"Yes, ma'am."

He opened the door for her and they entered the store. The aisles were narrow, so he slid his arm around her waist. She moved closer, her softness pressing against him. It was like holding her in the past, but better. She was less timid, less uncertain. She was a woman now, not a child. Just as he was a man, not a boy. What would it be like to love her fully now? To have the joys and pain of life blend to make the loving all the sweeter?

"What do you think?" she asked him.

He looked down at her upturned face, at the deep blue eyes that threatened to drown him, at the lips so full and soft and moist. He had thought he'd passed the age where hunger and desire eliminated all reason, but right now he felt eighteen again. He felt as if he were falling in love again. Or was it *still*?

"I think it's a little expensive," she said, "considering it would have to be refinished."

Refinished? He blinked, and realized they were standing in front of the table she had seen in the window. She was awaiting a coherent response from him. "Sure," he said.

"Sure?"

Obviously that wasn't coherent enough. "I mean, right. Whatever you say."

She gave him a strange look, then turned to the salesman. "I think we'll look around a bit more."

They spent the rest of the morning wandering through other shops while Rachel compared tables and he made meaningless comments. Finally, she decided the first table had been the best. They went back and bought it, along with a lowboy. Ben didn't care what they did as long as he was able to walk at her side and melt in her shadow.

"You know, I was wrong," he said around his roast beef sandwich a little while later. "I thought you'd just grown more beautiful since I saw you last, but you've also grown meaner. I could have starved to death while you fussed over a stupid table."

"It's a beautiful table," she corrected him. Her eyes were glowing. "I know it will look gorgeous in your office."

"Maybe *you* know it will," he said. "All I know is that my feet hurt and I was in danger of collapsing of starvation while you haggled over the price."

"Poor little Ben."

There was a tremor of laughter in her voice that

was like the coming of spring. It seemed to release something in him, pushing away his restraints. He reached across the table for her hand. "There are ways you could make it up to me."

Her eyes met his steadily. Her lips curved into a gentle smile, as if she knew her power over him. "By moving the furniture into place when it's delivered?" she asked.

"How vicious you've become," he said in mock despair, but their hands stayed locked together until it was time to leave the restaurant.

Six

"Have a good time," Laura called, even though her grandparents were already halfway down the block. "Boy, I sure hope Grandpa doesn't get into trouble."

"Trouble?" Rachel asked. She was tired, emotionally more than physically, from her trip to Galena with Ben, and Laura's words roused her from her half-sleep. "Honey, I've been to these functions myself. Believe me, an informal get-together at a trustee's home is hardly the atmosphere for a brawl."

"Some of the people who voted for Dr. Healey are going to be there," Laura said darkly.

Rachel's smile dimmed. Why this antagonism toward Ben? she wondered. "Hiring Dr. Healey was hardly an insult to your grandfather," she said. "He can't do the job anymore and he realizes it."

"They didn't give him a chance after his stroke."

Rachel opened her mouth to argue, but then

quickly closed it. What was there to say? Laura had her prejudices, and defending Ben would only reinforce them.

"What show do you want to watch on TV?" she asked, changing the subject with determination. "We have a choice between reruns, reruns, or more reruns."

Laura's grunt was close enough to a laugh, so Rachel didn't dispute it. For the next hour they watched television in silence. It wasn't an angry silence, but neither was it exactly companionable. Finally Rachel decided the television had put enough of a wall between them. It was time to open a gate.

"Want to tackle that cherry cobbler your grandmother made?" she asked when the credits of the show they had just seen were rolling across the screen.

"Sure."

They dished it up, then sat at the kitchen table. Why was Laura so hard to talk to since they'd arrived here? Rachel wondered. Or was she? Maybe it was her own preoccupation with Ben that had made conversation difficult.

"Your grandmother mentioned you met some kids your own age today," she said.

Laura shrugged, playing with a cherry that had rolled to the side of her plate. "Meg and Betsy Forrester. Their dad is going to teach math here."

"Are they nice?"

"I guess."

The conversation was going nowhere fast, and Rachel was relieved by the knock on the back

door. Anything to break this awkward silence. It
was Ben. A smile took over her lips and her heart.

"You left these in the car today," he said, holding out her sunglasses.

She let him into the kitchen. He greeted Laura
cheerfully; the girl returned a surly "hello."

Rachel sent her daughter a scolding frown, then
turned back to Ben. "You didn't have to make a
special trip with the glasses. I don't expect to
need them tonight."

"No trouble," he assured her, and glanced pointedly toward the table. "Uh-oh, lucky I came by.
You did hear there was a cherry cobbler warning
out for this evening, didn't you?"

Rachel set her sunglasses on a counter. "A cherry
cobbler warning?"

"It's a well-known fact that cherry cobbler at-
tracts vampires and should never be left uneaten
overnight."

"Oh, really? I sure hope you can help us eat this
then." Rachel was only too willing to join in his
silliness, but Laura wore a closed expression. Well,
Rachel thought, maybe this was a chance for Laura
to get to know Ben a little better, to form her own
opinion of him rather than blindly accept her
grandfather's. "Laura, would you get Dr. Healey a
plate?"

Laura did as she was asked, but there certainly
was no welcome in her manners. Rachel flashed
her a dark look which Laura ignored.

"So how are you enjoying Dubuque?" Ben asked
Laura.

"It's okay." She handed her mother the plate

and fork, then after a silent battle of wills looked over at Ben. "Would you like some iced tea?"

"Thank you, yes."

Aware of Laura's concession, Rachel rushed to cover the awkwardness. "She met the Forrester girls today. I guess their father's joining the math department."

Ben nodded..

Laura brought his iced tea and sat back down at her own place, fiddling with the remains of her dessert. "We're going to bike up to Eagle Point Park tomorrow," she said. She looked directly at Rachel, as if daring her to forbid it.

But why should she? Rachel wondered. She was glad to see Laura making some friends here. "Maybe Grandma can pack you a lunch."

"There's some great picnic areas there," Ben said. "You can have your choice of overlooking the river, the town, or a secluded grotto."

"Sounds spooky," Laura said, carrying her empty plate to the sink. "I like open places. I only agreed to go because Grandpa's going to the doctor tomorrow afternoon and Grandma said I couldn't come along."

"If you let yourself, you might have a good time," Rachel said.

"I guess." Laura stood hesitantly at the kitchen door. "Can I go watch television now?"

How would Laura get to know Ben any better if she was watching TV? Rachel wondered, at a loss between daughter and father. But would forcing Laura to stay solve anything?

"Sure, honey," she said.

"Good night, Laura," Ben called.

"G'night," she replied over her shoulder.

Silence fell between Ben and Rachel. The refrigerator made a sudden whirring noise, then ice cubes fell into the tray in the freezer. From the hallway came the chiming of the grandfather clock. Rachel pushed her plate back.

"I'm sorry," she said. "Laura usually has better manners. I'm afraid she's picking up her grandfather's bitterness."

Ben took her hand. It felt good, as if she weren't so alone. And that, in turn, felt dangerous. "Are you sure that's all she's upset about?" he asked.

Rachel stared at him. He didn't know; he couldn't know. "What else could it be?"

He looked at their hands, the fingers entwined. "We spent the day together and here I am again. Am I right in assuming that you haven't dated since David's death?"

"No, I haven't, but—"

"Children often have trouble seeing a single parent start dating."

She closed her eyes, waiting for the storm of emotions to pass. Was she dating Ben? They'd just escaped for the day, hardly a meaningful encounter in spite of what her heart was telling her. In spite of the hungers his kiss had awoken. But Ben wasn't just anybody; he was Laura's father.

"Yes, maybe you're right," she said.

"She'll get used to the idea," he said, and stood up. "Just give her time."

What did Laura have to get used to, though? Rachel asked herself. Her dating, or her dating Ben? She followed him to the door, not ready to part from him.

"You don't have to go," she said.

"Yes, I do. I have to prove to Laura that I'm not a threat, so I'll leave and you can go watch television with her."

"Do you know what awful shows are on this time of the summer?" Rachel asked, grimacing. "You're sentencing me to a fate worse than death."

Suddenly she was in his arms, in a paradise she'd been dreaming of, but it was better than her dreams. The world was filled with sunshine and laughter and Ben. There was nothing else but him as his lips met hers in a sweet explosion of desire.

She clung to him in wonder and delight, her arms sliding around his solid body to hold him as tightly as he was holding her. His mouth contin ued to caress hers, to plead, to offer, to tantalize her with the promise of splendor. She met his passion with a deepening one of her own. Could there be any other heaven but that which existed in his arms?

The refrigerator whirred again and slowly Rachel pushed away. The lights of the kitchen brought her back to reality. "I'm really getting wild," she said with a hesitant laugh. "Kisses in my father's old office and now in the kitchen."

Ben's eyes flamed with a hungry glow. His gaze locked with hers, the force of his desire holding her captive. She yearned for him, his touch, his kisses. She wanted to feel his body pressed against hers, bare flesh to bare flesh. She read the same longing in his face, then, abruptly, he released her. But the look in his tiger eyes told her what was between them was far from over.

"Want to have dinner with me tomorrow night?" he asked.

"Sure."

One of his fingers brushed her lips, then he was gone.

It took what seemed like several centuries at least for Rachel to begin to breathe again, and then several more before she could stand on her own, away from the support of the closed door. What had happened to her in these last few days? She felt as if she'd been bewitched. She walked to the table in a daze and reached for Ben's plate. A movement in the doorway caught her eye. Laura stood there. Rachel didn't need to wonder how long she'd been there. Laura's frown told all.

"Through watching television?" Rachel asked, uncertain which path to take.

"How can you throw yourself at him like that?" Laura asked angrily.

Obviously the easy way out was discarded. "Honey, I wasn't throwing myself at him. We were kissing, that was all."

"That was all!" Laura's voice was trembling. She sounded on the verge of tears. "You should see the way you look, all moony-eyed and sappy."

"Laura!" Rachel's crispness cut through the air. Laura sobered and held her tongue. A long moment passed while Rachel tried to find the words to make it all right.

"Laura." Her voice was softer, not pleading exactly but gentler. "David's been dead more than a year now. I get lonesome, even with you and Grandma and Grandpa around. I still sometimes need a man to hold me."

"But him!"

There was such venom in Laura's voice, such hatred, that it frightened Rachel. Ben was Laura's father. How could she hate him so?

"It's not Ben's fault that your grandfather had a stroke," Rachel said. "It's not his fault he was hired to replace Grandpa. If it wasn't Ben, it would be someone else. Your grandfather isn't strong enough to do the job anymore."

"I'd rather it was anybody else," Laura cried. "I hate him!"

"Laura! I won't have you saying such things!"

Laura said nothing. Her look of youthful insolence was streaked with fear. Rachel gazed steadily at the girl for a long moment, then looked away. Laura fled down the hall and Rachel sank onto a kitchen chair, depressed beyond words. How could she get Laura to like Ben, to see how good and special he was?

Ben was early the next evening for his date with Rachel. He hadn't been able to stay away any longer. Even waiting on the porch of her home was better than pacing his small apartment. Rachel's smile would make him forget the frustrations of his job, the battering-his-head-against-a-wall feeling that he had every time he tried to take a step forward. His knock was answered almost at once by Laura. She looked at him as she might look at a worm slithering across the wet sidewalk, but she let him in. He'd win a smile from her yet, he vowed.

"Hi, Laura. Your mom ready?"

"She said she'd be down in a minute. Grandma said to let you wait in the parlor." Laura obviously didn't want him to get the notion that courtesy was her idea.

"That would be fine. Dare I hope you'll keep me company?"

She didn't answer, but did perch casually on the edge of the sofa, ready to escape at the first chance. Lord, the girl really disliked him, he thought.

"So, how's school?" he asked.

"It's summer." Not only was he a worm, he was a dumb worm.

"I was trying to ask if you liked school," he explained carefully.

"It's okay."

Were two words at a time her limit? "What grade are you in?" he asked. "Sixth? Seventh?"

Her violet eyes reflected her disgust. "I'm going into high school," she said. "I'm not a little kid anymore."

High school? "No, I guess you're not."

How could she be going into high school already? he wondered. Not that he doubted her word. She did look more like a high schooler than a sixth or seventh grader. But that made her older and that, in turn, meant Rachel hadn't wasted any time in finding someone to take his place. It shouldn't bother him—it was a long time ago—but it hurt, as if the wound were still fresh. Hadn't their love meant anything to her? Had she just been a girl ready for rebellion and passion, and he had just been convenient?

Bitterness welled up inside him, leaving a sour

taste in his mouth. His anticipation of the evening died. He wished he hadn't asked her out. He wished he hadn't seen her again, that his dreams of a love that would last forever hadn't been resurrected. He wished he hadn't been touched by the vulnerabilty he thought he'd seen in her eyes.

"Hi, Ben. Ready to go?"

He turned to see Rachel standing in the doorway, looking beautiful in a rose-colored dress. Yes, rose was the perfect image, he thought. Beautiful, but painful for anyone who got too close.

"Yes, I'm ready," he said. He wouldn't let her know how close he'd come to getting hurt again.

The tires whined across the bridge to East Dubuque. Rachel's mood all day had swung from excitement over her evening with Ben to gloom over Laura's complete dislike of him. Why, when things had the chance to be perfect, did storm clouds have to block her sun? But she was determined not to let Laura's frown follow her all evening. She would have a wonderful time. She would find the magic that she knew lay in Ben's arms. She would weave her way back to the stars and ecstasy. Except that Ben seemed to have a different plan for the evening. His mood was less than joyful.

She turned to stare at his craggy profile. The tiger eyes were scanning the road. A frown lurked in the stern set of his jaw, even if it wasn't visible on his lips.

"A penny for your thoughts," she said.

He smiled over at her, but the smile didn't curl

her toes or weaken her knees. It was a polite, distant, nowhere-near-his-eyes smile. "There's nothing much there," he said.

Her toes froze with worry. "You seem quiet. Any special reason?"

He was concentrating on his driving and spared her only a quick glance. "No. Just thinking about the last time I was in Dubuque."

She thought of that time often, but the memories warmed her. They didn't put a chill in her eyes.

"I really loved staying with Uncle John," Ben went on. His voice became distant, dreamlike. "He was a lot of fun. We went fishing almost every morning. We'd be up before dawn, grab a quick breakfast, and then be down by the river just as the sun was coming up over the horizon."

This was his cherished memory of that summer? Rachel asked herself, stunned. What of the nights of love? The whispered words and the desperate embraces? Her heart pulled back in sudden fear. Didn't he feel the irresistible pull between them, the raging hungers she felt?

"We always caught a mess of bluegills," he continued. "Then we'd bring them home, clean them, and have fried fish for lunch. You remember things like that all your life."

"Oh." She stared straight ahead. What had happened to that teasing man she'd gone to Galena with? The one who had made her laugh, who'd held her hand and caressed her with his eyes? Had she dreamed all that? Had the last week awakened so many memories that she had imagined a tenderness that wasn't there? But what about those kisses? She hadn't dreamed them up.

The car began the long, torturous climb up the bluff to Timmerman's, the restaurant he had chosen, clawing its way through the narrow little streets. Rachel felt as if she were doing the same thing, struggling up the side of a cliff toward happiness, while Ben kept making the slope steeper. Finally they pulled up to the low white building that housed the restaurant. It rang with memories also.

"I imagine you had many a Sunday dinner here," Ben said as he turned off the motor.

"Yes." Something must still linger of their old enchantment, she thought. He could still read her mind.

"My uncle told me this was the only place for law-abiding, God-fearing Dubuquers to get booze on a Sunday."

Rachel was glad of the distraction. "I remembered Dean Healey as being a polite gentleman. Are you sure that's the same man you're telling these stories about?"

Ben laughed. "No doubt about it. He was Dubuque's premier schizophrenic."

She searched Ben's tiger eyes, hoping for a return of warmth along with his laughter, a return of that intimacy charged with awareness. But his gaze was as bland and calm as a field of hay on an early morning in June.

Once inside the restaurant, they were led to a table by the window. The view, though serene, was breathtaking. Below them, the Mississippi River was a sluggish brown snake winding its way to New Orleans. Across the river they could see Dubuque and, off to the north, Eagle Point Park. The giant oaks looked so small from here, Rachel thought. Ben ordered white wine for them both, and they sipped it in silence as they looked out the window. Ben still seemed miles away.

"How about a nickel?" she asked.

He turned, his eyes slowly focusing on her determinedly smiling face. "A nickel?"

"I offered you a penny for your thoughts before and that wasn't enough, so I'm willing to go up to a nickel."

He paused to drink some more wine. "There's nothing deep there. I was just wondering if you found this place changed much since you were here last."

And that lent such melancholy to his eyes? she mused. But she'd play his game until she could find the truth.

"I remembered coming here as a little girl and straining in my seat to see out the window. We usually sat over there." She gestured to a cluster of tables about a third of the way into the dining room.

"Didn't your father use his influence to get a table by the window?" Ben asked.

She shook her head. "He said it wouldn't be right to use his office in such a frivolous manner."

"I did."

He smiled, and for a moment she saw the flicker of emotion in his eyes, a brief return to summer before the chill came back. But even that momentary spark was enough to set her heart to racing. Was it Ben or the bluffs? she wondered. Maybe she should just stay away from high altitudes. Maybe she should stay away from Ben.

"Are you folks ready to order?"

Rachel stared dumbly at the smiling young waitress.

"I can come back later if you need a little more time," the waitress said.

They'd already had fifteen years, Rachel thought. "No," she said to the waitress, unable to keep sorrow from tingeing her words. "We don't need any more time."

They both ordered steak and baked potatoes. Salad with house dressing. Solid middle-America fare. The same thing Rachel and her parents used to order. She'd hit a time warp and returned to her childhood, she thought.

"You must have gone to college after Laura was born," Ben said.

Rachel turned back from the past, but Ben's eyes were distant again, miles and centuries away.

"Yes," she said. "I went at night."

"Anything special?"

She shook her head. "The arts. Mostly literature, English, that sort of thing." This was like a first date. A bad dream of a first date, where you made polite conversation while counting the minutes until you could flee. What had gone wrong? Things hadn't been this stilted yesterday. Their hearts and souls had raced with an urgency that was now only a distant memory.

"And you?" she asked back politely.

He shrugged. "Economics, law. I got a Ph.D. in economics."

Their salads came; they retreated into a pool of

silence as they ate. Laughter from other tables danced about in the background, but their gazes kept returning to the bluffs and the river, the eternal river. What had gone wrong? Rachel wondered. Why was Ben so distant?

"David must have been quite a man," he said suddenly.

She stared at him. Pulled from its cloud, her mind wasn't quite functioning yet.

"You'd always told me how strict your father was," Ben went on. "So David must have been quite a man to get your father's permission to marry you so soon after high school."

She hesitated. Ben didn't know a thing, and maybe that was the best way to leave it. "David was a very fine man," she said.

Her eyes closed briefly as she thought of David's inner strength, his courage, his insistence that she face the problems of the past rather than hide from them. Because of him, she would not run from trouble now. She faced Ben, her eyes meeting his squarely.

"We've talked mostly about me," she said. "How about the life and adventures of Dr. Benjamin Healey?"

"It's not really that interesting," he replied.

"Is that what you tell all the girls?"

"No. Usually I lie."

They both laughed, and their spirits inched closer together. Some of the ice melted from his eyes; some of her pain was pushed back into the past.

"Anyway," Rachel said firmly after her umpteenth sip of wine. "How was Dartmouth?"

"Hard to say," Ben admitted. "I spent only a week there."

Her breath caught. She was stunned. "A week?" she repeated. He had been gone when she'd written to him about her pregnancy?

"Yeah," he said slowly. "I just wasn't ready for college. I wasn't grown up yet, so I volunteered for a couple of years in the Marine Corps."

"So all the traveling around you said you did, the Orient, the Mediterranean . . ."

He smiled sheepishly. "I neglected to mention I was with the Marines at the time." His smile faded. "I don't mean to make light of it. It was a great experience for me, and really forced me to grow up."

Rachel was silent for a minute, staring hard at Ben. Somehow she'd decided that she and Laura were the only ones who'd suffered. Now she realized that these last fifteen years for Ben had been filled with just as much pain and joy and struggle. That knowledge made her humble.

"Did you go back to Dartmouth later?" she asked quietly.

"I went to Lawrence College in Appleton, Wisconsin, and then the University of Chicago. The whole time I was writing to my uncle here." He stared into his wineglass. "I found out who I was through him. I'm just a small town, midwestern boy. This is where I want to spend my life. Just like my uncle and your father."

Their dinners arrived, and again they ate in silence. They had known each other so well and yet there was so much that they didn't know, Rachel thought. After the plates were taken away, she stole a long look at the father of her child. It was strange. He'd grown much harder in the time apart, yet he had also grown much softer. He was gentler, more patient. She could sense the changes even if she couldn't see them.

"Would you like dessert?" the waitress asked. "We have some delicious cheesecake."

They both snapped their heads around to stare at the waitress, and Rachel saw that Ben looked as bewildered as she felt. They each turned down the offer of dessert and soon were walking across the darkened parking lot. Somehow they both paused at the same moment to look off across the river. There was a momentary flash of car lights in the darkness north of Dubuque.

"I guess Eagle Point Park hasn't changed," he said.

"I guess not."

"Kids sneaking up there, just more of them in cars now."

"Yes."

"Life goes on."

"Life goes on." She looked into his eyes, but in the pale light, the image was blurred. It was Laura she saw, not Ben. Life indeed went on.

Seven

Rachel stood by the window in her darkened room, staring out at the night-shrouded campus. Lights flickered here and there across the campus. Was one of them Ben's? she wondered. Was he returning to his room, as disappointed as she was that the evening had held no magic? Had he even noticed? Did he care?

She turned away from the window. What had gone wrong tonight? She had had such a wonderful day with Ben yesterday and had been looking forward to seeing him tonight. Why had everything gone sour?

Still dressed from their dinner at Timmerman's, she lay down on the bed and stared up at the squares of light thrown on the ceiling through the window. Ben had been almost playful yesterday, yet there had been a serious tone to much of what he'd said. How did she feel about her? Did he still feel the attraction, that hunger that pulled them together, that caused her heart to race and drove her wild with longing?

Their parting argument from years ago was as fresh in her mind as if it had happened yesterday. It had been a night much like this, warm with a slight breeze. The stars had been laughing and the moon had been just right for lovers.

"I've got it figured out," she had told Ben.

"Figured what out?" he'd asked.

She was locked in his arms. Her head was resting against his bare chest and the solid rhythm of his heart was the lullaby she wanted to lull her to sleep always. Her hand crept up to stroke the soft dark hair and moist skin of his chest, to feel the hard body that had been pressed against her minutes before in the overpowering hunger of their love. They were in the grotto, their special hideaway in the park. The breeze stirred the leaves so that the stars were playing hide-and-seek. The moon sent down a gentle glow. They were in a fairyland, a magical place where all their dreams could come true.

"I talked to Ruth O'Brien," she said. "She always gets her family's mail and said you could write to me there."

Ben pulled away. His sheltering arm, his comforting embrace was gone. She sat up, confused.

"I told you I'm not going to sneak around anymore," he said angrily.

"Ben, be reasonable."

"I'm tired of the dishonesty." He was on his feet. The wondrous moon was turning traitor and giving Ben light to find his shirt and shoes.

"And what's the alternative?" she cried. She

was frightened. She needed Ben. He was her life, her hopes, her dreams. "You know what my father's like."

"How could I know that? I've met him exactly four times, for a total of five minutes, and never once were you mentioned."

"Ben!" She stood up and stumbled on the stone floor of the grotto. "Please! You've got to understand! He would be furious if he found out how I care about you. He wants to lock me away in an ivory tower."

"How do you know that?"

She was afraid he was going to go, was going to walk away and leave her there. It wasn't the darkness of the park that frightened her, but the stubbornness in his voice. She touched his arm.

"Ben, please! I'll tell him, I promise. But let me pick the time. Write to me through Ruth for now."

He pulled away and walked to the edge of the grotto to lean against the stone wall. His shadow in the moonlight fell across her, long and unforgiving and unchangeable.

"Ben, I love you," she whispered. "Don't do this to us."

He turned, but his face was hidden in the darkness. His voice brought her no solace. "I'm not doing anything I shouldn't have done long ago. I want to come to see your father tomorrow before I leave for college."

"Tomorrow! You can't. Just give me time. I'll tell him, I will."

Ben said nothing. His eyes were unreadable in the darkness and long moments—an eternity—

passed. "Get your shoes, Rachel," he said. "You have to get back."

What did that mean? she wondered. Had he given up this righteous battle he wanted to fight? Was he willing to give her the time she wanted, the time she needed? She got her shoes and they left the park without speaking.

He stopped when they reached the library, their usual place of parting. "Well, Rachel, which will it be?" he asked. "Shall I come see your father tomorrow or is this good-bye?"

Her fear ignited into anger. There were some things Ben didn't know. In spite of his travels around the country and his high ideals, there were some things she knew better than he.

"It'll be neither," she said. "You can't come to see my father. He'd forbid you to write to me or see me again. If you love me as much as you claim to, you'll do as I wish."

His silence was heavy, weighed down by his scruples and his idealism, but she knew he'd see her point. He'd agree. He had to.

"Well, I guess this is good-bye then," he said.

Her heart wanted to stop, but anger kept it going. He was bluffing. "I guess it is," she said stiffly, and reached into her pocket for Ruth's address. She slipped it into his hand as she leaned forward to kiss his cheek. "Here's Ruth's address. Good luck at Dartmouth."

He was gone, but she was certain he'd be back. His train left tomorrow evening. She'd sit out in the gazebo tomorrow and he'd slip over to see her. He'd come around to her way of thinking.

All that last long day she had lain on the lounge

in the gazebo and nothing had happened. The bees had hummed, the dragonflies had swooped, and her eyelids had drooped.

When Rachel opened her eyes, she was alone in her bedroom. She swung her feet over the side of the bed and glanced at the clock. It was after three o'clock in the morning. She was no longer sixteen and Ben wasn't eighteen. And the magic had indeed gone with the passage of time.

"George, good to see you."

"Ben."

George Wickersham shook Ben's hand, then settled himself into a chair, turning slightly so the morning sun wouldn't be in his eyes.

Ben sat back down at his desk. "I was putting the finishing touches to our marketing program presentation. I just hope that everyone will listen with an open mind."

The elderly banker, who had been chairman of the college's board of trustees for almost thirty years, looked away from his view of the campus with seeming reluctance. Was the scene from this office in the administration building so enthralling, Ben wondered, or was George's alternative view not to his liking? Something was wrong; Ben could sense it. Who else was questioning the decision to retire Dr. Dupres now?

"You can relax," George said as he faced Ben. "I've canceled the trustees' meeting for tonight. The natives are too restless."

Ben took a deep breath and expelled it slowly.

"It's just putting off the inevitable. If they want Dr. Dupres back, I'll step down."

Ben pushed himself out of his chair and gazed out the window. He'd rather face his detractors and get this whole issue out in the open. If he wasn't meant to stay here, than so be it. The open road had been beckoning anyway. His dreams of Rachel had proven to have all the substance of smoke. Why not leave?

"You're not going to step down," George said. "All we're seeing now is a backlash of guilt. Nobody, not even Robert Dupres's doctors, expected him to make such a complete recovery, but that doesn't change the fact that the enrollment of the college is slipping. We need new blood and new ideas. The others will come around to our way of thinking in time."

Ben turned from the window. Why torture himself with pipe dreams of belonging? "In whose time?" he asked. "How long am I supposed to wait in this limbo?"

"I was on the board when we hired Dr. Dupres," George said quietly. "It was the best damn thing we ever did for this school, but the world moves on. Yesterday's heroes don't hack it today."

"He's built a beautiful institution here," Ben said.

"And if he remains as president, it will die."

"We don't know that."

"Be sensible, man," Goerge snapped. "To sell this institution in today's market is going to require a man with a fire in his belly." He smiled slightly. "Speaking from personal experience, I can assure you that after a certain age that fire burns with considerably abated intensity."

Ben did not reply.

"I'll reschedule a meeting of the trustees for next week," George said. "My secretary will call you with the date."

Ben just nodded, then turned back to the window. The door behind him shut quietly. The silence of the room was haunting, mocking. Would he ever find the home he'd wanted for so long? Did it matter if he stayed here or left if he was to face the challenges alone?

He wanted to go to Rachel, to confide his frustrations to her and find them eased just by the sharing. Yet, who was she? Had the girl he had thought he had known, the girl who he had thought loved him ever really existed? After Laura's revelation of her age last night, he wasn't sure. The Rachel he had loved wouldn't have been able to replace him so easily. Irritated with himself as much as with her, he strode from his office.

"I'm going for a walk," he told his secretary.

"Be careful, Dr. Healey," she called after him. "The sun is dreadfully hot."

"I'll be fine."

He had no destination in mind, but his feet took charge, carrying him across the campus, through a residential area, and down to the riverbank opposite the locks. Sitting on the grass, he began throwing stones into the water. A small splash followed by ripples that radiated out to die. Over and over. A splash, then ripples.

Why had he told Rachel that stupid fishing story

last night? This spot along the river was certainly burned into his memory, but it wasn't fishing that he remembered. He remembered coming out here every evening and arguing with himself about seeing Rachel. She was willing to meet him at night on the bluffs above the river, but she wouldn't take him home to meet her parents.

A burning sensation stung his eyes. He rubbed them to ease the irritation. She apparently had known something, because her father still didn't want to see him.

Oh, hell. Ben threw the whole handful of stones into the water. Ripples fought ripples, then they all died. Why was he sticking around anyway? For Dr. Dupres, Rachel, any of them? This place had been nothing but trouble back then and that was all it ever would be. It didn't hold the answer to his dreams.

He rose and brushed off the seat of his pants, knowing that all of this was foolish bravado. The talk of leaving was nonsense. His heart had broken the last time he'd left. He wasn't going through that pain again. It was time he stayed and fought for what he wanted. If Rachel hadn't loved him enough back then, it didn't matter. He would make her love him now.

Sometime during the near sleepless night Rachel had given up. Whatever she and Ben had had in the past was gone. Even the friendship she had hoped for seemed impossible, if their dinner at Timmerman's was any indication. But she'd lived most of her life without Ben. Continuing to do so should be no problem. There was no reason for her to feel so depressed.

She and her mother tackled the parlor that day, spending the morning wading through boxes of photographs. There were Rachel's old school pictures. Family photos. Sixteen shots of her and her parents by their Christmas tree, one for every year she had still been living here. She had no such shots of Laura. There had been no camera at Laura's first Christmas to begin the annual recording of the passage of time. She hadn't had the money for a camera and later, when she had been married to David, she had never gotten into the habit of taking pictures. There were some, but now, after it was too late, she wished she had more pictures of David and Laura, more tangible reminders that Laura had had a father.

Jessica stopped sorting to fix lunch, leaving Rachel alone with her thoughts. She and Ben might not have any future, but Ben and the college did, she told herself. It was time she stopped moping and did something about her father's stubbornness. She went up to his room.

"Want some company?" she asked her father as she entered the room. When he smiled and nodded, she sat on the edge of the ottoman. "You missed your regular game of chess with Laura this morning and I thought you might want a game."

"Might as well," he said.

She set up the pieces. "Mother was showing me pictures of the retirement village. It looks very nice."

Her father stared at the chess board. "The Eskimos handle it a lot better," he said. "When their old people are no longer productive, they put them on an ice floe and push it out to sea. They die fairly quickly that way. Our society likes to hide their elderly in so-called retirement homes and drag out the dying process." He moved a pawn to start the game.

"Burlington is a lot closer to St. Louis than Dubuque," Rachel pointed out. "We'll see more of each other."

Robert said nothing, and Rachel forced herself to concentrate on the chess pieces. She moved her knight.

The silence was uneasy. Her gaze kept flickering between the board and her father. "We still have a lot of packing to do," she finally said. "I imagine you have some loose ends to tie up also."

"Like what?" he growled. "Watching some punk kid get fawned over by a bunch of stupid old trustees?"

She ignored the bitterness. "There must be a lot of things that you need to cover with Dr. Healey. You know, teacher contracts, programs you've started, that kind of thing."

"Laura told me you've been spending time with him. I should have known you'd go over to his side." Laura's venom was mild compared to that in Robert's voice. Rachel's impatience spurted into anger.

"I haven't gone over to anyone's side," she said, then took a breath to calm down, to ease the irritation from her voice. "This isn't a matter of sides, it's a matter of doing what's best for the college. Do you want the programs you've worked so hard to build to fail just because you're too stubborn to explain them to someone else?"

He glared at her, his eyes afire. He was ready to fight. "The man throws me out of a job and you're seeing more of him than me."

Rachel vowed to stay calm, to stay in control. She would have her say. For Ben's sake. "That's not true, Dad. Besides, Ben and I are old friends. Isn't it normal that we should enjoy each other's company?"

"How many of your other friends from high school have you called?" he demanded.

"Dad, I'm tired of all this. I had nothing to do with the board seeking a replacement for you after your stroke, and neither did Ben. Why are you taking your anger out on us?"

"Why are you flaunting my replacement in my face every chance you get?"

She stood up. She was trembling inside and hoped it didn't show. It had been fifteen years since she had courted full-scale war with her father. She faced him squarely. "I've had enough, Dad. I'm tired of the way you blame everybody for the fact that you're just getting older. I think it's stupid that you've devoted your whole life to this place and are ready to jeopardize everything because of some immature stubbornness. But most of all, I don't like what you're doing to Laura. She's just a kid and doesn't need to share your bitterness or your hatred. Be sad if you want. Be nostalgic, but stop turning my daughter into a hateful, intolerant little monster."

The words came out stronger than Rachel had intended, and the silence following them was all the more deadly. Her father didn't move. He didn't breathe. She walked out of the room, certain she hadn't helped Ben at all. If anything, she'd probably made her father more angry and vindictive.

Eight

Lunch was a silent affair, but Rachel wasn't sure who was being more stubborn in refusing to speak, her or her father. Regardless, she was glad to escape to the parlor to sort through more photographs, though her thoughts were hardly a pleasant companion. How had life turned around so suddenly? Just yesterday afternoon everything had been perfect. Her world had been blissful and Ben had seemed within reach.

Then, out of the blue, he was within reach again. He was standing before her with a huge bouquet of roses.

"To make up for being such lousy company last night," he said. The old light was back in his eyes and the teasing note in his voice.

"You weren't lousy company," she protested as she buried her face in the fragrant blossoms. Her crazy heart was singing with joy. "I had a good time."

"We could have had a better time."

She met his eyes, but the fire in them almost scorched her and she had to look away. What was he saying? Did he want to try again, or was her overactive mind conjuring up her own dreams?

"I've got an appointment with the registrar in a few minutes, so I can't stay," he said. "I just wanted to give you these flowers and ask you to give this to your father." He handed her a letter typed on official college stationery.

"It's not your resignation, is it?" she asked in fear.

"Hardly," he said with a laugh. "I'm just asking him to see me later in the week."

Her heart began beating again. "I tried to talk to him, but he wouldn't listen. I think I probably made matters worse."

"I doubt that." He leaned over and kissed her lightly, yet the touch was enough to wash away her depressing memories and replace them with an insistent desire for more of him. But he was already walking back to the door. "I have more tricks up my sleeve," he said, "so don't worry if he refuses my request. In the end, this will all be settled."

How? she wondered.

He pulled open the door and turned to touch her again with his smile. "I always get what I want."

Always? she wanted to ask. And what was it he wanted? But he was gone already and she wasn't sure she would have had the nerve to ask anyway. She found a vase for the roses and went back to sorting through the photos, but the room was filled with the scent of Ben's flowers and her heart could not help but swell with happiness.

Ben came by the next day with a picnic lunch. "It's too nice a day to stay inside," he said. "Go get your daughter and let's wade through the fountain while we eat."

"Ben, you're insane," Rachel said, but she was laughing and her heart was singing with happiness. Life was bright and beautiful again. "I'm not wading in the fountain with you."

"Ah, so you're afraid." Passion flared in his eyes. "You know how powerful the fountain water is. You're afraid it will make you fall in love."

"I don't want to risk catching a cold," she said, though that was a ridiculous protest on such a hot and sultry day.

He moved a step closer. Her stomach turned a somersault and her lungs forgot how to work. "I'll let you off for now," he said huskily. "But one day soon, we're going to test those waters."

His voice held a challenge, softly made, but there all the same. What did he want from her? Her memories of the past were getting too mixed up with the present and she couldn't think straight. "I'll go get Laura," she said, and slipped by him to go upstairs.

Laura wasn't pleased by Ben's invitation. "I don't like picnics," she said, which Rachel knew was a blatant lie. How many times over the years had Laura pleaded with her to take their lunch to the park a few blocks from their home, or even to eat in their backyard?

"It won't hurt you to spend an hour with Dr. Healey," Rachel said. Besides, she needed Laura's protection. Her overactive imagination was producing dreams even when she was awake. "He thinks you don't like him," she added.

"I don't."

"Laura, you're coming with us and you're going to be polite." Rachel had had it with her daughter's rudeness.

The girl got to her feet slowly. A trip to the dentist would have been greeted with more enthusiasm, but Rachel figured Laura's surliness could be her anchor. With Laura's frown only half-hidden, Rachel would be able to keep her feet firmly planted on the ground, no matter what she thought she heard in Ben's voice. They went down the stairs.

"Hi, Laura," Ben said, smiling.

"Hello."

A breeze off the coast of Antarctica would have more warmth than Laura's voice, but Ben gave no sign that he noticed and ushered Rachel and Laura outside. "I'm afraid I've got a meeting at one," he said, "so we can't go anyplace exotic."

"Like Eagle Point Park?" Laura asked.

He laughed. "If that's your idea of exotic, your mother has kept you too sheltered."

"That's the last thing she needs to be told," Rachel said. "She's already been pushing to start dating."

"In groups, Mom," Laura explained. This was a familiar refrain in their ongoing argument.

"Laura, this isn't the time or place for this discussion."

Laura turned to Ben. "Don't you think I'm old enough to start dating?"

"Definitely not," he said.

Rachel laughed at his vehemence and at the look of frustration on Laura's face, but a twinge of sadness pulled at her. They were bickering like a family. Unknowingly, Ben sounded like the father he was.

"But it's not fair," Laura went on. "Mom wants to keep me locked up so I never can have any fun."

Ben smiled over Laura's head at Rachel, the sunshine in his eyes dimming slightly. "This sounds like the same argument you used to have with your father."

Laura's head came up, her gaze pinning Ben. "How would you know that?"

"Dr. Healey and I are old friends," Rachel said, intercepting Laura's suspicion. She was glad the campus was deserted and no one was around to overhear. "As I recall, I used to complain loud and long to anyone who would listen about my father's injustice."

"So you admit you aren't being fair," Laura said.

"I admit nothing." Rachel frowned at her daughter. "I was sixteen when I was having those arguments with my father. You're only—" She stopped, unwilling to tell so much. "You're still younger. When you're old enough to date, I'll let you. I promise."

Thankfully, Laura let the matter drop and they continued on to the fountain in silence. The water caught the glitter of the sunshine and winked at them, inviting them to relax. Rachel remembered so many summer days when she had longed to wade through the fountain's coolness, but had never dared. During her father's reign, no one waded in the fountain. A few people had, herself included, fallen in love without its help anyway.

"Want to give it a try?" Ben asked.

Falling in love again or wading? She wondered. "I thought you were offering us lunch," she said, avoiding the subject.

They sat down on the edge of the fountain and Ben opened the bag he'd been carrying. "I want you to remember I made this myself, so be kind."

The sandwiches were peanut butter and jelly. "Some treat," Rachel teased, denying the little voice within her that said it was certainly a treat. Just being here with him, getting to know him again . . .

"How come you haven't married, Dr. Healey?" Laura asked, biting into her sandwich.

"Oh, never met the right woman at the right time," he said lightly. His gaze flickered to Rachel, then away.

She was not looking for love, Rachel firmly told herself. She was back here in Dubuque to see her parents. But if love should happen, if love should stray her way, she'd grab it with both hands and never let it leave again. She took the carton of grape juice Ben handed her and settled her feet more firmly on the ground. No more wild fantasies, she vowed. They were strictly for impressionable teenage girls.

"In an effort to be healthful," Ben said, "I also brought carrot and celery sticks, apples, and potato chips."

"Potato chips?" Rachel asked. "A new kind of health food, I take it?"

"My kind," he said, laughing as he ripped open the bag of chips. Rachel was pleased to see Laura take a few. That was all she wanted to happen. Laura had to get to know, and like, Ben.

"You know," Laura said, "I would think somebody who liked kids enough to work at a college would be married with kids of his own."

"I don't deal that directly with the students here," Ben explained. "It's more a management and marketing position. Selling the college to prospective students, prospective donors, and alumni with fond memories. And I don't know about these students here, but when I was in college I didn't consider myself a kid."

No, Rachel thought, he hadn't been a child back then. Then she pulled her mind back to the here and now. She didn't want to inch down again those dangerous paths to the past.

"Does the campus look very different from what you remembered?" she asked, choosing a safe, neutral subject.

"Smaller," he said, and they both laughed.

"Most of the changes don't seem to be too visible from out here," she said. "The science labs have been modernized and computers are everywhere, but the buildings all look the same."

"Just a little older, a little more ivy on them."

"I guess that's what time has done to us all," she said.

"Put ivy on us?" Ben asked, and even Laura laughed.

"No," Rachel said. "Most of our changes are

inside. We may look pretty much the same as we did years ago, just a little grayer, but inside we may be very different people."

"What's she trying to tell me?" Ben asked Laura, leaning conspiratorially closer to her. "Has she been computerized?"

Laura nodded and reached for another handful of potato chips. "Right. She's a bionic mom."

"No wonder she's so good at moving furniture."

"She's good at lots of stuff." There was a touch of defiance in Laura's voice, even a hint of anger.

Ben's teasing grin disappeared. "I'm sure she is," he said quickly.

The mood of the picnic had changed once again, and Rachel was relieved rather than sorry when she looked across the campus to the clock tower on the library. It was getting close to one and time to go. Ben walked them back to the house. The silence of the campus was depressing this time.

"It was fun," Rachel said. She looked at Laura pointedly.

"Thank you for inviting me," Laura said. Or recited rather, for it sounded like a lesson being played back. She was being resentful once more.

"We'll do it again soon," Ben promised.

Laura ran inside, but Rachel lingered on the back porch with him. "I'm glad you included her," she said.

"Did it do any good?" He gave a short laugh. "I can't figure out why she dislikes me so. Most people find me boringly respectable. Could that be the problem?"

"She's coming around," Rachel assured him.

"She ate your food and talked to you. It must mean she's starting to like you."

He took Rachel's hand, holding it gently, yet firmly enough not to let her go. His thumb moved against the inside of her wrist, a hypnotic, sensuous caress. "You ate my food and talked to me. Does that mean you're starting to like me too?"

She wanted to pull her hand away. His touch was too pleasant, too tempting, and had started a tingling warmth creeping up her arm. She wanted to flee before it crept into her heart, but when she moved her hand slightly, his grip tightened.

"Ben, don't be silly."

"How am I being silly?" His voice was innocent, holding only childlike confusion, but the gleam in his eye was another story. A tiger was resting there, watching his prey. "If you don't like me, but ate my food anyway, I want to know. I don't want to waste my terrific peanut butter and jelly sandwiches on an unappreciative audience."

"I like you," she said uneasily. "You know that."

"Sure, but the question is, how much do you like me?"

He moved closer and his eyes seemed to possess her. She was awash in sensations, the musky scent of his aftershave, the taste of his lips, the power of his embrace. But no, those were just memories. Or were they dreams of what she wanted now?

"Do you like me more than pineapple juice?" he asked.

"What?" She stared at him, puzzled, unprepared for his silliness.

"More than apple pie? More than baked potatoes? More than corn on the cob?"

"Well, I don't know about that last one," she said with a laugh.

"Ah, so that's my rival." He brought her hand up to his lips. His kiss burned, and that tingling warmth was no longer creeping along. It was speeding to engulf her whole body. "Now that I know, I'll do my best to wipe it out."

She was lost in the sensual spell he was casting. Her breath came in gasps. "Iowa's been a corn state for a long time. I'm not sure they'll want to change."

"I have powers untold."

That she knew. Her weakened knees, her racing heart, her treasured memories of the last few days all told her that.

He let go of her hand, but brushed her lips with his before she had time to move away. "Want to go wading in the fountain tonight?" he asked.

"Ben." She stepped back from his touch, back from the potent strength of his gaze, back into sanity. "You're going to be late for your meeting. I'll see you later."

"Spoilsport." But he left and Rachel fled inside. Eventually her heartbeat slowed to normal and her lungs remembered how to work. She joined her mother in cleaning out the kitchen cabinets and didn't even try to talk to Laura until she had herself back under control. She got her chance to be with her daughter when the two of them were doing the laundry in the basement later that day.

"Did you have a good time at lunch?" she asked Laura. The girl tossed a blouse and a shirt of her grandfather's onto the pile of white clothes. "I thought you and Ben got along pretty well."

Laura started loading towels into the washing machine. "Grandpa told me I had to be polite."

"And was it that hard to do?" Rachel handed the girl a towel that had dropped and Laura tossed it in the washer. "Ben's a pretty easy guy to get along with."

"I guess." Laura had grabbed the detergent off a shelf and was making a career out of pouring it into the measuring cup.

"Give yourself half a chance," Rachel said, "and you might find that you like him."

Laura looked up. "Mom, I promise to be polite, but don't expect anything else. I'm never going to like the guy."

Laura sprinkled the powder over the towels and Rachel started the machine herself. It would take Laura another lifetime at the rate she was moving.

"Why not?" she asked. "What is there about him that you dislike so?"

"I can't explain it," Laura said. She fiddled with the detergent box, a transparent excuse not to meet her mother's eyes. "I just don't trust him. He pretends to like people, but I don't think he really does. He's pushed people aside, he's hurt people, and he doesn't care."

Rachel took hold of Laura's upper arms, gently turning the girl to face her. She had to make Laura understand. "Honey, that doesn't make any sense. First of all, Ben didn't push your grandfather out. The board of trustees retired him, and then hired Ben. Two separate actions. Ben had nothing to do with your grandfather's retirement.

And you're wrong when you say Ben doesn't care. He knows this is very hard for your grandfather and wishes there were something he could do to make it easier."

"Oh, Mom, you just don't understand!" Laura cried, and leaned wearily against the washer, breaking Rachel's hold on her.

"No, I don't," Rachel admitted. She looked at the stubborn set to Laura's face, the hint of righteous indignation in her eyes. Ben had looked the same years ago—and days ago—whenever he was stirred up about something. Couldn't Laura feel the pull of a kindred spirit?

"Laura," Jessica called down the stairs. "Meg Forrester is here."

Laura looked up. She was just a child, confused and hurt and angry. Rachel reached over and mussed her daughter's hair. "Both you and your grandfather just need more time. Go have some fun and stop worrying."

Nine

It was easy enough for Rachel to tell Laura to have some fun and stop worrying, but almost impossible for her to follow her own advice when Ben came by after dinner the next evening.

"How about if I take you and Laura to the movies?" he asked. "I'll even promise double helpings of popcorn."

Rachel's silly heart did a few cartwheels at the smile in his eyes. But when she went upstairs to tell Laura, the girl's reaction drew clouds across the sunshine.

"I'm tired, Mom," she said. Her yawn was almost believable. "I was thinking of going to bed early."

For the first time in about ten years Laura was choosing to go to bed early? Rachel thought, sighing with discouragement. How could she get Laura to see how special Ben was? To see the goodness that he believed in? She wanted to order Laura to go with them, but what would that accomplish? More resentment, most likely. She trudged back down the stairs to where Ben was waiting, wondering if she was being wise with her patience or cowardly in running from a confrontation.

Ben took Laura's refusal in stride, and Rachel reluctantly went along with him. As much as she wanted to be with Ben, she couldn't bear to see Laura troubled. Hadn't she hurt Laura enough in the past?

"I don't know, Ben," she said as the two of them strolled along the quiet streets toward the theater downtown. Her heart wanted to sing at being close to him, but Laura's eyes kept drowning out the song. "Maybe I shouldn't be going either."

"And how will that make her like me better?"

"Things are just moving too fast. Going out with you once a week would be one thing, but we've been seeing each other every day. Maybe I should be spending the time with her rather than with you."

"Rachel, she's had you for years, and right now you're with her all day. A few more hours isn't going to make a difference."

"I don't know. Maybe to her it seems like I'm spending all my time with you. Maybe that's why she's misinterpreting the seriousness of our relationship."

"Is she?"

Rachel wasn't going to pursue that line. It was another one of those paths she didn't dare explore with Ben. She wanted to be friends with him. She wanted Laura to grow to like him. That was all she was hoping for. The weakness in her knees, the dreams of him that haunted her sleep, meant nothing more than that once they had been bound together. She wasn't really looking for love; she wasn't really looking to repeat the past. No matter what her heart said; no matter the fever that burned in her at his touch.

They walked in silence past neat frame houses with families sitting together on the front porches. Children threw balls in the yards, rode bikes that had been turned into motorcycles by playing cards clothespinned to the frames, and played freeze tag and hide-and-seek. Everywhere around her and Ben was the laughter and love of families. A deep ache in her heart told her she wanted to be a part of it, a part of it with Ben and Laura. So much for her brave ideas of uninvolvement.

Across the street from them, a father was teaching his toddler daughter to play catch with a big red ball. Over and over he'd throw the ball. The little girl would squeal in delight as she waved her chubby little arms in a futile attempt to catch it. When Laura had been that age, around three, she hadn't had anybody to squeal and play with. Rachel had been trying to make ends meet while going to night school at the local junior college, and just hadn't always had the time or energy to play.

"Time isn't a gift always given," Ben said, calling Rachel's mind back to the present.

"We had lots of time back when we were teenagers," he went on. "But we didn't realize how precious it was. Now we've only got a few weeks before you go back to St. Louis. That doesn't give us much of a chance to get to know each other again."

For once Rachel forced her thoughts into words. "But for what purpose?" she asked. "Our lives are too far apart. What's the urgency of rekindling our friendship?"

"Friendship wasn't all we shared."

No, it wasn't. But the memories of those nights were bittersweet. Along with the ecstasy had come the agonizing pain of loneliness. She had no desire to repeat that again. "I think we've grown beyond Eagle Point Park," she said dryly.

They had crossed the street, leaving the warmth and laughter of the homes behind as they passed former houses that had been turned into insurance offices and accounting firms. Washed clean of family chatter and front lawns, the buildings seemed empty and forlorn. She concentrated on the sidewalk and the few cars passing on the street, wishing she and Ben were back amid the houses and families. The air seemed to take on a chill here.

He reached for her hand, forcing her to stop walking and look at him. "I wasn't talking about sex," he said sharply. "I was talking about the relationship we had, the feelings we had. I thought it was special, something to cherish and worth searching for again. Was I wrong?"

She had thought it was special, too, but what did he mean "search for it again"? "No, you weren't wrong," she said after a long moment.

Next to them was a low wall enclosing a parking lot, and Ben led her over to sit on it. She kicked absently at the fine gravel at the wall's base, trying to put her fears into words. When she glanced at Ben, she saw in his eyes the boy she had loved. But she no longer felt like the girl she used to be; she felt old and tired and afraid.

"Going back again isn't possible," she said. "We can't wash away the years that have passed."

"I never said I wanted to." He took her hand again, sheltering it between both of his. "For the sake of all we've shared, I want the chance to find out who you've become. Maybe we'll find friendship; maybe we'll find more. But I think we deserve the chance."

"Oh, Ben." He didn't have the slightest idea what this "chance" could cost him or her. Yet could she rightly say she wouldn't see him anymore?

He lifted her hand to his mouth and kissed its back, then turned it over and pressed a kiss against her palm. She held her breath as excitement tingled through her. Without thinking, she lifted her free hand and raked her fingers through his thick hair, urging his head to rise. He looked at her, and the fire blazing in his eyes seemed to melt all of her hesitancies and doubts.

"Rachel," he whispered, and leaned close to kiss her. She welcomed him gladly, twining her arms around his neck as his tongue flicked across her soft lips.

The kiss deepened as their lips parted, and they explored each other with the same feverish passion that had driven them as teenagers. Only the sudden sound of a car engine revving called them back to sanity, and reluctantly they pulled away from each other.

Wordlessly, they stared into each other's eyes.

Rachel was shaken by her response to Ben—and by the deep emotion his kiss inspired in her.

"Like I said," he murmured in a low voice, "what we had is worth searching for again." Suddenly he grinned. "And I think I'm going to enjoy the search."

She laughed with him, and let him help her off the wall. As they continued, hand in hand, to the movie theater, Rachel couldn't help thinking the search, for her, had already ended. She had the giddy and despairing feeling she had already fallen in love with him again.

The boat rocked gently under Rachel's feet as she stepped off the gangplank, her hand firmly held in Ben's. "You know," she said, "when I was little I thought this was the most marvelous restaurant imaginable." She gazed around the old paddle-wheel boat turned supper club. "I always wanted to come here for my birthday, but my father didn't think it was suitable for a child. Besides, it was open only for private parties."

"It still is," Ben whispered as the tuxedoed maître d' approached them.

"Welcome to the *Delta Dream*," the man said. "Your hospitality committee has cocktails being served upstairs. We'll be leaving the dock in a half hour, and then dinner will be served. Dancing is after that."

"Sounds great," Ben said, nodding his thanks to the man. Taking Rachel's arm, he moved her away as the maître d' greeted the next couple.

"Our hospitality committee?" she whispered. "What is going on?"

"Nothing. I knew you'd like this and arranged to get us tickets on its next cruise."

"With what group?" she asked, eyeing the elderly couple eyeing them.

"Oh, I can't quite remember. The reunion of one of the senior high school's graduating classes."

Another older couple caught her eye. "Ben, we don't belong here."

"Sure we do." He patted her hand as they strolled toward the gangway leading to the upper deck. "I bought tickets for us. They hadn't sold enough tickets to the alumni and had offered the rest to the general public."

On the upper deck they found the bar. A banner that was hanging over it welcomed the senior high school class of 1947. Rachel wanted to die of embarrassment but, sure enough, she and Ben were expected. They had blue and white nametags awaiting them and a table assignment.

"You two sure look well-preserved," one of the hospitality committee joked as he handed them glasses of punch. "Were you really in our graduating class?"

"Only as a twinkle in our parents' eyes," Ben said.

The older man laughed. "Oh, I get it," he said with a knowing look. "You're hoping the moonlight and the dancing under the stars is going to melt this little lady's heart, right?"

Rachel's cheeks burned slightly, not from the older man's words but from the knowledge that Ben already had her heart. Moonlight and dancing hadn't been necessary to win her over, just his touch, his smile, his caring ways.

"I thought success was guaranteed when I bought the ticket," Ben said.

The man laughed. "Nope, just the setting. It's up to you to do the rest."

"I promise to do my best," Ben vowed, but he was speaking to Rachel. His warm look embraced her.

"I'm impressed already." Her words were soft, floating on the evening's gentle breeze.

"Just wait. After an evening of moonlight and romance, we won't need to walk through the fountain."

Who needed that old fountain anyway? she thought. But she just smiled a silent acknowledgment of his teasing tone and they walked to the side of the boat to watch the preparations to leave the dock.

The fire in Ben's eyes no longer frightened Rachel. It warmed and consumed her, but old cautions were hard to throw off. Rather than risking being lost forever in Ben's spell, she turned and watched the river as the boat pulled away from the dock. She pretended to be impressed with how quickly they left land behind, with the view of the meat-packing plant, with the bridge they were about to pass under, but her mind wasn't on any of those things.

Was it only ten days since she had returned to Dubuque and found Ben again? Was it only last night that she had realized how much she still loved him? Time had become a whirlpool, spinning her, pulling her in, until the passing hours and days seemed to have little meaning. It was just Ben, Ben and the magic he was weaving around her.

Yet even that wondrous enchantment wasn't without a shadow of worry. How could she get Laura to share in this joy? Were time and gentle understanding all she needed, as Ben thought? Was it possible for all the past hurts and misunderstandings to be wiped away, leaving no trace for future hauntings?

"I think we're supposed to find our table," Ben said.

He took her arm and led her back to the lower deck. The gentle swaying of the boat kept them pressed close together, but the boat had nothing to do with the warmth that was ever growing between them, with the hunger for Ben's embrace that dominated her every thought. It wasn't the moonlight that made her see desire in his eyes, or the breeze that made her skin crave his touch.

They found their places at the end of a table for eight and were soon drawn into conversation by the older couple next to them.

"We were sweethearts in high school," the woman told them, "and then we drifted apart."

"But never again," the man said. "We were lucky enough to find each other again and we're not letting go."

"Must be something in the air," Ben whispered into Rachel's ear. Maybe it was, she thought. Or at least in the air that night. She could almost believe that time was no barrier to their love.

She had a wonderful time. Dinner was a blur of steak and wine, seasoned with the sound of laughter around them and the warmth of love. Ben's eyes, his touch, kept her in a constant state of heightened emotion. She wanted him back in her life, and here, amid the romance and charm of the evening, it began to seem possible. All the problems could be solved; none were insurmountable.

By the time dinner was over, it was dark. The moon lit a path down the river for the boat to follow. The stars were their guides. Toward the front of the boat a band started playing sweet old love songs, and Ben and Rachel joined other couples in dancing. The boat's lights dimmed and the strings of tiny Italian lights that hung around the edge of the dance floor came on.

"It's like Christmas," Rachel said. "A magical, warm Christmas."

"There's a magic here, all right," Ben said. "But even my Christmases never felt this good. I've never been as happy as I have been this last week with you."

She knew what he meant, and melted farther into his arms. The music wove around them, drawing them closer together. The night was theirs to explore the fantasy of their love, to dream impossible dreams that would surely come true.

They danced and danced, their mutual embrace a haven of peace, of security, of promises untold. Her hunger for him grew, but so did her deeper need for him. In his arms, life seemed a riddle easily solved. Problems could be washed away by the sunshine in his smile; rest and contentment were attainable only in his arms.

Rachel awoke from her love only when the band stopped to take a break. Other couples wandered back to their tables, or to join old friends. Rachel and Ben climbed the steps to the upper deck, but avoided the crowd around the bar to wander to the back of the boat.

It was darker there. One other couple was locked in an embrace on a bench, and she and Ben walked to the railing overlooking the paddle wheel. It splashed with a steady rhythm, the heartbeat of the evening. Behind lay a trail of spilled diamonds, the gleam of the stars as the river settled back into slumber.

As they watched in silent rapture, the boat turned around. The water churned in distress as the boat started its journey back up the river to the dock.

"It's half over," Rachel said sadly. The magical night had been so special. She didn't want to see the end approaching.

"No, it's just half begun," Ben whispered. "It doesn't ever have to end."

She turned to find his arms waiting for her and went into them. He kissed her as no one had ever kissed her before. The earth stopped. The sun, the moon, and the stars gave up, and love exploded to light the world in their place. Life and everything sweet and wonderful gave itself up to him and her love.

She held him close, as close as a whisper, as close as a promise of forever. Her lips sang of love and belonging and sweet blessed nights beneath the summer sky. How could life be anything without him? How could laughter exist without the sun of his touch to make her smile?

Their mouths spoke as lips were crushed together. It was the summer. It was the night. It was then, yet it was now. Love and need and unbearable longings merged, flowing like waves upon Rachel's soul. She needed Ben more now than she ever had in the past. She needed his touch, his passion, his gentle understanding. She wanted to be held, to have life be more than waking and sleeping. She wanted it to shout with excitement and joy, her heart to rave with the pure oneness of spirit with another.

"Ready to wade in the fountain tonight?" he whispered.

"Fountain? What fountain?" she asked. She rested her head against his heart, her heart. The solid rhythm of his love enclosed her. "We must have already waded."

"Maybe so," he murmured, and his lips claimed hers again.

It was time to stop pretending. Love had found them once again.

Ten

"You're going out with him again, aren't you?" Rachel's father asked her one afternoon. It was a week after the silent Timmerman's dinner, five days since Rachel had discovered she was still in love with Ben, and four nights since she had abandoned worrying about the future. Take things as they come, she had decided. Whatever was to happen would happen.

"Yes," she answered as she idly watched her father and Laura play chess. "Ben should be here any minute now." Though she had grown closer to Ben in the past week, he had made no progress with her father. Every day he left a letter, and every day her father ignored Ben's request to meet with him. "We're going to the Alpine Music Festival in New Glarus."

"Grandpa says it's going to storm," Laura announced.

Rachel looked out the window. The sky was

clear, the sun warm. This felt like a repeat of their first night here. Hadn't they progressed any further than that? But then, this whole visit felt like an endless time warp, spinning her from years ago to the future, then back to last week.

"I hope your rain holds off until morning then," she said.

"It won't," her father said. His voice was definite, as if he were not willing to give any hope.

Rachel bit back her impatience as Laura's back stiffened. No, she was not going to get into any arguments tonight, about the weather or anything else.

"I guess we'll just have to bring umbrellas," she said lightly.

"Won't do much good with the downpour we're going to have," Robert said.

"I think you should just stay home," Laura added.

Rachel turned back to the window. Would the sniping never end? Here she was, head over heels in love with Ben again and Laura still couldn't bear the mention of his name. Over and over in the past week they had invited the girl to go with them, only to be refused most of the time.

Chess pieces clicked sharply against the board. "Ha," Rachel's father cried. "Caught you there, Miss Smartie."

"Grandpa. Don't gloat," Laura chided. "You know I wasn't paying attention to this game."

Rachel caught a glimpse of Ben as he came up the walk. "Ben's here," she said. "You sure you don't want to come with us, Laura? It's not too late to change your mind." She stood and picked up her sweater and purse.

"I'm positive. Grandpa and I have lots planned for this evening." Laura didn't even look up as she set out the pieces for the next game.

"We do?" Rachel's father sounded puzzled. "I can't see how playing chess and watching TV is more exciting than an outdoor music festival."

"I like chess," Laura insisted.

"So do I," he said. "But I'd sure find some other time to play if I had the chance to go to that festival with your mom and Dr. Healey."

"Grandpa, you would not."

Rachel frowned at the byplay. What was her father up to? "Well, you two behave," she said slowly. "I'll be home late."

"Oh, Rachel." Her father's voice caught her half-way through the door, and the following silence rang with worry before he spoke again. "I was just thinking. Maybe you should invite Dr. Healey to dinner tomorrow. There really is a lot I should cover with him before I leave."

Astonishment froze Rachel. "Dad?" she squeaked.

"Grandpa," Laura protested.

The doorbell rang. Her father was setting up his pieces for another game and Rachel knew he wouldn't explain his statement either to her or to Laura.

"Thanks, Dad," she said. She returned to kiss his cheek and thought she detected a twinkle in his eye, then flew down the steps to greet Ben.

It was a night for celebrating. Both Rachel and Ben felt it. Her father's invitation was part of it certainly, but there was something else, some other tension in the air that made her shiver with delight. The two-hour drive to the music festival seemed to pass faster than the blinking of an eye. Somehow between the need to watch Ben, to hold his hand, and to marvel in the strength of his presence, they arrived at the park without her being aware of it.

Rachel knew they had talked during the drive, but she couldn't remember any of the words. Their eyes had been communicating other things— warmth, need, tenderness—while their hands had reached out for the other's, the current of love flowing between them.

The park was moderately crowded, but they found a clear spot on the grass under the shelter of a wide oak. Ben spread out the blanket he'd brought and, as the orchestra warmed up over in the bandshell, he unpacked the picnic basket. Champagne first.

"How'd you know my father would give in tonight?" Rachel asked as Ben popped the cork on the bottle.

"Who says I brought the champagne to celebrate that?" His smile was a caress, his voice an embrace. "Can't we just celebrate being here together?"

"Why not?" She laughed and took a glass from him. Their eyes met even as their hands brushed, sparking the embers into a steadily growing flame.

They relaxed in the growing dusk, eating cheeses and iced shrimp and sipping the champagne as music swirled around them. Speaking more with their hands than their voices, they rediscovered the magic Rachel had thought belonged only to being sixteen and in love.

Halfway through the concert, the stars disappeared behind the clouds, but the rain held off for almost another hour. Then, to the last strains of a German folk tune, the picnickers all grabbed up their blankets and baskets and scrambled to their cars as the sprinkles rapidly progressed to a torrential downpour. Both Rachel and Ben were soaked by the time they fell laughingly into his car.

"Father was right about the storm again," she said. "I may never hear the end of it."

"Nothing wrong with a little sprinkle," Ben said. His voice was soft, yet filled the car.

"No," she said. The pounding rain surrounded them, blocking out the cars around them, enclosing them in darkness and wonder.

"Think how glad the farmers will be," Ben whispered. His voice was hoarse.

"I'm so glad for them."

It was too dark for her to see him clearly, but her body could feel his hunger. Her mind could sense him reaching out for her. She went into his arms gladly, hungrily.

Their lips met and the world spun. Was it the storm or was it Ben's touch? Rachel didn't know and didn't care. It was all one and the same.

His kiss was raw, raging desire. It was a visit from the past, but it was different too. His lips begged for her softness and her warmth, while he surrounded her with strength and power. He touched, he sought, he delighted. They weren't teenagers anymore. They were adults, with adult hurts and needs and tenderness to share.

Headlights slashed across them and they pulled apart. Their breathing was ragged, their hearts raced in unison. The car behind them beeped impatiently.

"I guess it's our turn," Ben said, and started the car.

"I guess."

She wanted it to be their turn. Not to leave the parking lot, but to find happiness. To find the dreams they'd shared years ago and to turn them into reality. Surely if his love was as strong as hers, they could solve the problems ahead. Her father, Laura, telling Ben the truth about Laura. All her troubles wanted to crowd into the car with her and Ben. They wanted to push out the warmth and magic of the evening and weigh her down with worries. But Rachel locked the door of her mind against them. Tonight was hers and Ben's. Tomorrow would be for worrying.

They followed the other cars back to the highway, but the steady downpour kept them from making much progress. After an hour, they were barely ten miles from the festival grounds. The tension that had seeped in with them wasn't the sort that tingled toes, but froze them. Rachel had all the faith in the world in Ben's driving, but not nearly as much in the cars that would suddenly appear out of nowhere and careen by before disappearing again into the storm.

"I think we're going to have to stop," Ben said. "Maybe we can find a restaurant and have some coffee while we wait for the rain to ease up."

But the restaurants were few and far between, and those they did pass were closed. Finally a light loomed ahead in the distance. A motel.

"Not what I had planned," Ben said wryly. "But it'll have to do. Even at the risk of your father canceling his dinner invitation, I'm not driving any farther in this storm."

"My father will understand," Rachel said with more assurance than she actually felt. "It would be dangerous to push ahead now."

Ben pulled up to the motel office and ran inside, leaving Rachel alone with the rain, the darkness-splitting neon sign, and her thoughts. Would her father understand? Would Laura? But she and Ben truly had no alternative. The rain was coming down in sheets. It was what her father would call a real gully washer. She could barely make out the words of the sign flashing at the end of the motel's driveway. There was no way they could drive home in this.

A rap on her window caused her to jump. It was Ben, water streaming down his face. He signaled for her to open the window.

"They have only one room available," he said. "You can have it and I'll sleep in the car."

"Don't be silly," she said. "Get in there and register us and let's get out of this rain."

His mouth opened and then closed.

"Get us a room, Ben." She rolled up her window to end the discussion. "Men," she muttered. The front of her skirt and blouse were soaked from just the few moments she had had the window open.

Soon Ben came running back out and jumped

into the car. Every square inch of his clothes and skin were soaked. Neither said anything as he drove to their unit.

"I'll go ahead and open the door," he offered.

Rachel pulled off her sandals, watching as he raced across the sidewalk. A beam of light high-lighted the door, beckoning to her. She hopped out of the car and ran to the room. Splashing her bare feet in the water made her feel like a little girl. She was laughing as she flew into the room.

There was one double bed in the small room and a combination dresser/desk with one chair. A stan-dard Wisconsin vacationers' special, she thought. The room didn't allow for anything besides sleep-ing. Her laughter died as a slow, seething warmth took its place. Well, there was one other thing they could do besides sleep. . . .

"I'll put some towels over here by the wall," Ben said. "And I'll use the coverlet for a blan—"

"Would you get out of those clothes?" she said sternly. The air-conditioning had been left on and she was already shivering from the cold. "You're going to catch pneumonia."

"I was just trying to get our sleeping arrange-ments straight," he said. "I hadn't planned this, you know. I don't want you to think that—"

"Get out of those clothes," she ordered as she turned off the air-conditioning.

Her heart was pounding loudly enough to chal-lenge the thunder. She and Ben were alone to-gether. All she could think of was the promise of delight, and here he was, playing the noble knight!

She turned back to him. He hadn't moved, and was frowning at her.

"You have three seconds to get out of those clothes and into a hot shower," she warned him. "Or I'll rip them off."

She almost hoped he'd stall and give her the pleasure. His tiger eyes darkened as he stared menacingly at her, but running barefoot in the rain gave a girl courage.

"One," she counted.

His eyebrows rose in challenge.

"Two."

He moved quickly, but with dignity, and slammed the bathroom door shut behind him. Rachel found herself chuckling as a feeling of power warmed her. Tiny rivulets of water easing down her face reminded her that her hair was wet. She wiped the drops away and walked over to the phone. She called home and her father answered.

"Dad, we're stranded by the storm," she told him. "We probably won't be back until morning."

"I told you it was going to rain."

"I know. I should have learned to listen by this time."

There was a silence, then her father spoke more softly. "I'd rather have you home safely in the morning than driving through the storm," he said. "It's got another several hours before it'll pass, so stay put until it's safe."

"We will, Dad. Give my love to Laura and Mom." And make Laura understand, she added silently, hanging up as a sharp rap sounded on the outside door.

"Towels," a voice called.

Rachel opened the door to a figure in a yellow

raincoat and rainhat. Thongs were on her ample feet.

"I brought you some more towels," the woman said. "They're extra large beach towels."

"Thank you." Rachel took the large bulky garbage bag from the woman.

"I also brought you a snack," she said. She handed Rachel a tray that contained half a cherry pie, plates, forks, and two cups, and two little pouches of instant coffee. "You can heat water in the bathroom," the woman added.

"Thanks so much," Rachel said, and closed the door.

She placed the tray on the desk, took a large towel out of the plastic bag, and knocked on the bathroom door. "Ben," she called. "I have some dry towels for you."

"The door's open," he called.

That wasn't the answer she'd expected, and she stared at the door, her heart pounding. In her mind she saw him in the shower, his body sleek and muscular as the soap suds and water cascaded over it. His skin, his hair, would gleam wetly, catching the light, catching her gaze. She swallowed hard and reached for the doorknob, but then dropped her hand when her courage failed her.

"I'll leave them on the floor here," she said, and ignored the quiet laughter from inside the bathroom.

The room was silent except for the pounding of the rain on the roof and the occasional sound of cars passing on the highway. Rachel sat on the bed, waiting for Ben. Uncontrollable desire ran rampant throughout her body, turning her blood to molten lava and her hands to ice. Would a piece of cherry pie keep her from going mad?

She got up to stare out the window, but could see nothing except the streams of water racing down the glass. Behind her she heard the bathroom door open. That would be Ben getting his towels. Half an eternity later she found the courage to turn around, and her heart shifted into overdrive. The large towel wrapped around his waist accentuated his sculpted body, his flat stomach and muscular chest with just the right touch of hair down the middle. Even the man's knees were fantastic.

She swallowed hard. "How does it fit?" she asked.

His dark green eyes were like the rolling waters of a stormy sea. "You tell me."

How could she tell him anything without revealing her love for him? It was too newly discovered to share, to expose to the harsh light of day, or night. She chose a cowardly retreat rather than chancing something in her eyes or voice betraying her.

"I'm going to take my shower," she said. She eased by him into the sanctuary of the bathroom and shut the door behind her. Solitude did nothing for her racing heart. "Don't eat all the pie," she shouted through the door.

She needed a leisurely bubble bath to relax and soothe her and bring back her common sense. She needed someone to remind her that she was an adult now, not an irresponsible teenager who could spend a passionate night in a man's arms and never consider the cost. But all she could think of was Ben and the bed out there and the long night ahead of them. She wanted him, needed him with the same intensity she had in the past. No, it was even stronger now. There was more to hide from in his embrace, more reason to rejoice in finding closeness, and more pleasure to be gained now in giving.

But there was no relaxing bath awaiting her. The plastic shower stall couldn't be called a tub in anyone's imagination. She washed quickly and let the cool water cascade over her, hoping it would cool more than just her skin. Afterward, she put on her beach towel like a sarong.

With a deep breath that promised bravery but didn't deliver it, she opened the bathroom door. Steam cascaded ahead of her, so the bedroom should have felt pleasantly cool. Instead, the air seemed just as supercharged as before. She could have melted one, if not both, of the polar ice caps.

"How does it fit?" Ben asked smoothly.

There was no need for a retort, clever or otherwise. His tiger eyes told her exactly how well her towel fit. The earth stood still and Rachel could feel herself falling into an eternal abyss of silence.

His gaze locked her in the doorway. He slowly came closer, then bent his head. "I'll make the coffee," he whispered, his breath stirring the few dried hairs by her ear. "You set the table." He nodded toward the single wooden chair, which was now by the bed with the tray on its seat, then slipped by her into the bathroom. As she started to walk away, he spoke again.

"Rachel."

She stopped in midstride. "Yes?"

"You cut the pieces, I get to choose."

Surprisingly, she relaxed. A fever of anticipation burned through her, but it was what she wanted. This night of magic, this night of glory. She cut the pie into two, and set one slice and a fork on each plate. Ben finished making the coffee, then sat on the floor.

"This isn't what I had planned," he said.

"I know." She handed him the larger piece of pie. "But we're stuck here, so we might as well make the best of it." That came out stranger than she had planned, and her gaze locked on her own piece of pie. "I mean, there's no reason to feel ill at ease."

He took her plate from her, captured her hands, and gently pulled her down to sit on the floor next to him. The warmth, the safety of his grasp made her feel confident again. The courage of running barefoot through the puddles had gotten all used up. She needed his strength.

"Relax," he said. "Nothing will happen that you don't want."

Ah, but what if she wanted something to happen? "I know that," she said, ignoring her wanton thoughts. "I don't want you to feel that just because we're here together that . . ." She tried again. "That just because we used to . . ."

"Relax," he repeated. The laughter in his voice brought a nervous smile to her face. The pie he handed her made her laugh out loud. "Eat."

They ate in silence, avoiding each other's eyes. The pie was good, but it satisfied only the hunger in her stomach. After she finished the last bit, Rachel laid her fork aside and picked up her cup of coffee. Ben didn't eat his crust and left his coffee untouched.

"I've thought about you a lot," he said suddenly.

"Oh?"

"I mean, before we met again. I wonde. ~d what you had done, where you'd gone."

The silence seemed to offer an invitation. Tell him, a voice cried. Tell him he has a daughter. But her mouth couldn't voice the words. Who had the right to know first, him or Laura? It was too big an issue to resolve here and now, and not with the presidency of the college hanging in the balance.

"I missed you too," she said lamely.

Somehow her foot brushed his leg. The touch scalded her, but she couldn't draw away. Oh, how she wanted him. It had nothing to do with the past. It was now, it was today. The yearnings of yesterday were a mild echo compared to her desire now. She needed him tonight, needed to feel alive in his embrace, to come awake under his caress.

"Really pouring out there," he said.

She nodded. "Lucky we found this place."

Their gazes met, darted away, then slowly slid back to feast on the other. The tiger in his eyes growled its hunger, yet somehow promised earth-shattering peace and contentment, strength and security.

But she was afraid, afraid to give herself to him again. She was afraid to love him as completely as she had in the past. Those hurts had never really healed. Still, she couldn't run. She couldn't hide. Ben was her destiny. Her life.

"Ben." It was statement, a question, a plea of longing.

He moved slowly toward her. His lips took hers. It was a gentle touch that promised much, the easing of hurts, the softening of pains. Then his mouth brushed hers again, this time telling her of joys they could share, of unchartered lands they could explore together. His breath was warm against her skin, his lips sweetly enticing her desire while soothing away her fears. How could she not love him, this magic man who could shake her to the depths of her soul?

Love was all they needed, all that really mattered. All that had ever mattered. Her heart was smarter than her head. It knew that Ben would always be a part of her life, always be a part of her.

His arms moved slowly around her, offering her security but also the heat of his fire. Her body seemed to ignite beneath his touch. Her breasts were crushed against him. Her love, his knowing touch, her overpowering needs sang a song of sweetness and ecstasy.

His hands were on her back, urging her ever closer. Her own arms encircled him, her hands delighting in exploring the smoothness of his skin, the rock-hard muscles that were her safety and her joy.

She touched his chest. The hair was wiry, his body solid. With her eyes closed, she spun back in time. The rain on the motel roof dissolved into the wind in the trees. She touched, she explored, she brought the fires within him to a raging pitch that only she could satisfy.

"Oh, my love," he gasped, awakening her anew to the powers she still possessed, the cravings that still drove him.

He loosened the towel that hid her body. His lips burned a trail from her neck to her breasts. With his mouth he worshipped her, his kisses and caresses tormenting and delighting her until she wanted to cry out. In splendor, in agony, in pure passion and need.

But even as his lips drove her to a rapturous peak, his hands slid down her waist and lower. They sought the warmth between her legs, knowing just the teasing touch to cause her to arch and pull him ever nearer.

"Rachel," he breathed. A question was in his eyes. "Rachel, take me back to heaven with you."

It seemed such a silly thing to ask. Together was where they belonged, and, yes, it had been paradise, hadn't it? Her lips clung to his, begging and giving at the same time. How had life ever seemed bearable without Ben's laughter? Without his passion?

"Oh, Ben, how I've missed you!" It was a sigh, a breath carried on the wind. She had no idea if he heard her, if she'd even spoken the words aloud, but something drove him harder, faster, to bring her fires of need to full conflagration.

He swept her up into his arms, and her towel fell to the floor. "I love you so," he murmured as he laid her on the bed. "You're the very heart of me."

His hands were possessive, knowing just what to do, just where to touch her until words, thoughts, were impossible. They clung together, locked in joy as hunger and needs and love beyond imagining engulfed them. She held him to herself, pulling him into her warmth, her core, the center of her being, and they again became one in body as they had been one in spirit for so long.

Together they rode the memories of yesterday into tomorrow, their love exploding into sound and wonder and light. A symphony of delight, of blazing lightning and crashing thunder, then, locked within each other's embrace, they fell back down to today. But even the falling was sweet and wonderful and something to cling to as sleep crept over them.

Rachel awoke to the feel of Ben's hand on her thigh. She opened her eyes to find his tiger gaze ready to engulf her.

"Good morning," she whispered, and slipped her arms around his neck to hold him close. The hair on his chest brushed her breasts, making her feel alive. And hungry. "Don't I know you from somewhere?"

"Perhaps." His lips attacked the smooth skin of her neck and shoulders. His touch was light, like the kiss of an early morning sun, yet left a burning on her. "Aren't you the lady who shared her cherry pie with me last night?"

"Ah, that must be where I've seen you before."

His hands moved into the shadow between her legs while his mouth slid down her shoulder to her breasts. His tempting caresses awoke the rest of her, the desires that had still been sleeping, and a sudden fire consumed her. Her hands roamed over his broad chest, his flat stomach, then danced lower to enflame him even more.

"You're better than hot English muffins to wake up to," he murmured.

"Such compliments," she said with a hoarse laugh. "Stop before I get an inflated ego."

His stroking touch had purpose. It brought delight, warmth . . . and overwhelming desire to share all of herself with him again. She had no power to stop him, no wish to tempt his hands elsewhere.

"Do you really want me to stop?" he whispered. His hands slowed teasingly.

"No."

His mouth claimed hers in a ravishing kiss that drove coherent thought far away. Then his lips moved down, finding flickerings of wonder on her neck. Her breasts came alive with just the slightest teasing of his tongue.

Then his hands grew bolder, demanding more. They swept along the length of her entire body, pausing here and there until she was clinging to him, her own hands claiming him as hers. When she had convinced him of the urgency of her hunger, he moved over her and possessed her completely with fierce tenderness and magic. The world spun and collided with the stars, then slowly stopped its whirling as they collapsed into each other's arms. Time stood still, then caught up with them.

"You know," Ben said as he shifted to lie beside her, "I sometimes think it's a miracle we found each other again." He traced a finger over her stomach. "And after all that time, to still feel the same way, it seems impossible."

She let her own fingers play amid the hairs on his chest, unable to move much, to think or even dream beyond the glory of his loving. "We're lucky."

He sat up, his tiger eyes flaring with sudden intensity. "Let's not leave anything to luck anymore. Rachel, I love you. Marry me."

Her dreamy lethargy fled; her sleepy wonder disappeared. "Marry you?" Wasn't it what she had dreamed of long ago? And not just long ago, either. Her wild flights of fantasy had taken her to his arms and back into his life as soon as they'd met again. Yet now, when his eyes sought hers, all she could see were the problems, the reasons keeping them apart.

"I don't know, Ben," she said. The glory, the fire of his embrace vanished, and she swung her legs over the side of the bed. Maybe the thin, worn carpet would inject sanity back into her.

He grabbed her hand to keep her from escaping. "You love me. I know you do," he said.

She stayed on the edge of the bed, reluctant to linger so close to the paradise of his smile, yet unable to wander too far from it. Her eyes met his for a moment. "Yes, I love you," she admitted. "But that's not the only thing we have to consider."

"That's all that's really important."

She shook her head and stood. The night had been for Pollyanaish certainties and magic. The daylight was harsh enough to burst the strongest bubbles and expose the magic for the trickery it really was. She picked up the beach towel she'd worn last night and wrapped it around her again.

"No," she said, "love isn't all that's important. There's Laura and my father and the college—"

Ben was out of the bed and gripping her upper arms before she could say any more. His eyes held her as much as his hands did. "If we love each other, we can make all those other things work," he said. "Laura just needs time to get to know me, to get used to the idea of you with a man other than her father."

Oh, Lord. What a mess. Rachel wanted to sink into Ben's arms for comfort; she wanted to run and hide; she wanted to cry.

No, she wanted to share this man's life. She wanted to risk the happiness she saw promised in his eyes, the happiness she'd found so briefly years ago. But she owed Laura the truth first. Laura, whom Rachel's selfishness had hurt in the past. No matter how much she loved Ben, she had to think of Laura first this time.

"Ben, I have to talk to Laura. I can't make this decision now."

He pulled her into his embrace and she rested her head against his solid chest. The steady rhythm of his heart should have brought her peace and contentment, but it didn't. All she felt in his arms was fear—fear that she would lose everything that had come to mean so much to her in the past few weeks. Fear that the truth would destroy her world.

"You can't let Laura make this decision for you," he said. His hands were rubbing her back, weaving a spell that pulled her closer.

She jerked away from him, afraid of his touch that kept her from thinking. "I didn't say she would," she protested, and reached for her towel. "I just need to talk to her before I say yes or no. The world's spinning too fast for me right now."

"Too many years have slipped through our fingers, Rachel. We can't afford to lose even a second."

"I know," she said. Her fingers fumbled with the knot of the towel. "But we moved fast fifteen years ago. A jet fueled with passion. And . . . and my world turned inside out. I have to take it slow this time."

"Okay." He kissed her ever so sweetly, the touch of a gentle mist. They showered, got dressed, and drove back home.

Eleven

The ride home seemed unbelieveably quick. How should she tell Laura about Ben? Rachel wondered. What should she tell Laura? After all these years of silence, she didn't have any idea how to start.

But then Ben was pulling up in front of her parents' home and the time for planning her talk, for choosing her words, was over. "Want me to come in with you?" he asked.

"No." She shook her head, though she hated to leave him. Away from his side, the fears could overwhelm her. "I've got to see Laura alone."

She started to climb from the car, but Ben's hand on her arm stopped her. "Hey, gorgeous!" he said softly.

She turned. His eyes—Laura's eyes—were dark with concern.

"Remember how much I love you," he said.

"I love you too," she whispered.

He leaned forward and kissed her, giving her hope and strength and the promise of happiness to come. A smile was in her heart and on her lips when he pulled away from her. It would be all right, she thought. Laura would grow to love him too.

"I'll see you tonight for dinner," he said.

She nodded and got out of the car. A smidgen of her courage left with him, but enough stayed to keep the smile on her face as she went into the house. She found her mother in the kitchen.

"Hi, honey," Jessica said as she looked up from the cookbook she was paging through. "Did you have a nice time at the concert? Such a shame that you got stranded."

"Yes, to both," Rachel said absently though she wasn't at all sorry she had spent the night with Ben. "Where's Laura?"

"Out back, I think." Jessica peered out the back window. "Yes, there she is in the gazebo." She smiled at Rachel. "I remember you spending hours out there every day in the summer too. Like mother, like daughter, I guess."

"Right." Rachel forced a lighthearted laugh, then went outside. Laura was lying on her stomach on the lounger, her chin resting on her crossed arms. Sunglasses hid her eyes. She didn't move even when Rachel sat on the chair next to her. Was she asleep?

"I'm awake," Laura said abruptly.

"Oh, good," Rachel said, though she wasn't sure it was. Where was she to start? With each passing moment, the silence grew thicker, a wall too high to see over and too wide to batter down.

"We had a nice time last night," she said finally, then her cheeks flamed when she realized what she had done last night. Laura made no response and just continued staring away, lost in rapturous appreciation of the library's south wall.

Rachel made another attempt to dent the silence. "Looks like you and Grandpa were right about the rain again."

Still Laura didn't stir, and Rachel's hands twisted together in agitation. How had she and Laura grown so far apart in the past two weeks? They'd never had so much trouble talking before. There had never been this solid barrier of determined disagreement. But then, Rachel had never tried to overcome fourteen years of silence and tell Laura who her father was, either.

Smiling bravely, she thought she might try melting the silence since she didn't seem able to knock it down. "If I had taken your forecast seriously and warned Ben, we would have made it home last night."

Laura turned at that. Her eyes were still hidden behind those mirrored glasses, but her lips were twisted in sarcasm. "Come on, Mom, you can't be that naive. I may be just starting high school, but I know what boys are after."

"What does that mean?" Rachel asked, though she was almost afraid to hear Laura's answer.

Laura sat up, tucking one bare foot under her. Her hair fell forward over her shoulder, making her look too world-weary for a fourteen-year-old. "It means that all men are out for is a little fun. If that storm hadn't come along so conveniently, your Dr. Healey probably would have had car trouble."

"That's a terrible thing to say!" Rachel exclaimed. She wasn't upset at Laura's tone, for her voice had been more resigned than vicious, but at the fact that Laura could think such things about her father. "Ben's not like that!"

"Oh, no?" Laura leaned forward, grabbing Rachel's hands in hers. "Mom, I love you lots, but let's face it. You're not a good judge of men. Even David saw that and worried that if something happened to him, you'd fall for the first smooth-talker that happened along."

Rachel was getting annoyed. "Ben is hardly a smooth-talker—"

"Mom, he's a user. He takes what he wants from people and goes on his way. He doesn't care who gets hurt." Laura spoke as if she were older, the wiser of the two of them. As if her heart had been broken and was held together with scars of cynicism.

The dull pain in Laura's voice evoked sympathy in Rachel, and that pushed out the remnants of irritation. She shook her head slowly. "Laura, I want you to like him. Can't you try?"

"No."

Laura pulled her hands away and looked out across the yard. Her back was stiff, her manner unyielding. She was the stalk refusing to sway in the wind, childishly believing it was better to break while holding fast to her views rather than to bend with compromise. Such youthful conviction, such obstinance, was all part of Ben's legacy to her. Why couldn't Laura feel the bond?

"He's a good and gentle person," Rachel said. "He cares about me; he cares about us."

"Oh, Mom, you believe anything anybody tells you," Laura cried in exasperation, and got to her feet. "David was right to worry. You do need someone to watch out for you."

"You have to give Ben a chance." Rachel was quietly insistent. "You have to stop being so stubborn and refusing to see anything good about him. It's important, Laura. He's asked me to marry him." She hadn't meant to blurt it out so, but Laura didn't look shocked.

"Oh, really?" she said scoffingly. "Was this before or after you got Grandpa to agree to see him?"

"Laura, that was uncalled for." Rachel was on her feet also. Anger and hurt warred within her. "I demand that you apologize."

"Apologize? Never. But what I will do is make sure he doesn't hurt you again." With that she took off, flying down the gazebo steps and toward the library.

"Laura." Rachel started after her, then stopped, knowing she had no chance of catching her. Laura was fourteen and running barefoot; Rachel was thirty-one and in loose-fitting sandals. She'd have to wait until Laura cooled off and came back home.

She turned toward the house, Laura's angry words echoing in her mind. Suddenly she froze in panic. Laura had promised to make sure Ben didn't hurt her again. Again? What in the world could she be referring to? Laura couldn't know. There was no way she could possibly know about the past. Was there?

Rachel spun around, her gaze searching the

campus frantically, but Laura was no longer in sight. What was she going to do? Whatever it was, it would backfire, Rachel was certain of that much. Laura was a child, a hurt and frightened child who would only end up causing more pain. Rachel couldn't wait leisurely at home. She had to find Laura and find her fast.

A quick cup of coffee was all Ben took time for, then he dressed and hurried over to his office in the administration building. His first appointment was with three of Dr. Dupres's supporters on the board, but with a little luck he'd be both on time and able to convince them to give him a chance as president. And good luck was certainly something he could depend on lately.

Hadn't he found Rachel again, made her love him, and, hopefully, want to marry him? As for Laura, he had no doubts that she'd come around soon. She was a nice kid, he could see that, but was going through a difficult stage right now. Once she got used to the idea of a new father, she'd be fine.

He opened the door of his office, and stopped in surprise. Laura and his secretary were in the midst of a furious argument. Helen saw him first.

"Oh, Dr. Healey," she cried as if a savior had appeared. "This young lady has been demanding to see you. Maybe she'll believe you when you tell her that your schedule is quite full for the day."

He just smiled at Laura though. "I'm sure we can make time for her," he said. "I believe I have a few minutes before I'm due to meet with the trustees."

Laura's mouth was grim; she made no pretense of returning his smile. Though her eyes were hidden behind sunglasses, there was an aura of anger and tension about her, and Ben's heart sank. He hadn't expected her to hug him with delight when she heard he wanted to marry Rachel, but he hadn't thought her reaction would be quite so negative.

"Come into my office, Laura," he said, and ushered her inside. The room seemed deathly quiet once he closed the door. "Would you like anything to drink? Some lemonade? Soda?"

"No, thank you." She sat in one of the large chairs across from his desk. Ben followed her lead, walking around his desk to sit in his own chair.

"How are you?" he asked.

"I'm fine, thank you," she replied, though it was obvious she wasn't.

Her hands were clutching the arms of the chair tightly. She seemed like a coiled spring about to explode. He wished she'd take off those sunglasses so he could see her eyes. He'd be able to tell what was bothering her when he wasn't staring at twin reflections of himself.

He waited for her to speak, but when she didn't, he asked, "What can I do for you?"

She stared for a long moment at the rug, her bare toes rubbing it. Then she looked up. "That first evening Grandmother said that you had been here before."

Grandmother? Ben repeated silently. Laura

looked cute and warm like Rachel. He couldn't imagine her saying *Grandmother*. Gran or Grandma would be more like her.

"Yes," he said, pulling his mind back to her question. "I spent a summer here with my uncle. He was a dean at that time. That's sort of like a vice-president."

"I know what a dean is," she said coolly.

"Sorry." He laughed it off. Laura had brought a tension into the room that was stifling him, trying to stop his run of good luck, but he refused to acknowledge it.

"Was that fifteen years ago?" she asked.

Her mouth was a straight line and Ben felt his own smile slipping away. "About that, I guess."

"How can it be 'about that'?" she snapped. "It was either fifteen years ago or it wasn't."

He raised his brows at her impatience, but forced a comment back from his lips. He would answer her concerns, would put her worries to rest, even if he didn't understand what she was getting at. He thought a moment, mentally counting back. "All right, it was fifteen years ago. So what?"

"Did you—" She hesitated, then took a deep breath. "Did you know my mother then?"

He gestured helplessly. What did this have to do with marrying Rachel? "Yeah, sort of."

"Did you do things with her?"

"We might have. Fifteen years is a long time, Laura. It's hard to remember everything I did that summer."

"Did you two make out?"

What kind of question was that for a daughter to ask about her mother? If only Laura would take off those damn glasses. He picked up a pen, staring at it as he twisted it around in his fingers.

"Some things I don't remember," he said. "Other things are . . . are just personal."

"Sometimes personal things don't stay just personal."

Irritated, he gripped the pen in both hands and looked up. "Laura, I really don't—"

She'd taken off the glasses finally, but her eyes weren't the dark violet he'd come to expect. Blue-green eyes stared accusingly at him. Blue-green eyes that were filled with tears.

"Laura?" he asked. He didn't understand.

But Laura wasn't in the mood for quiet explanations. She stood and braced her hands against the edge of his desk as she threw angry words at him. "I know all about you," she cried. "I know how you hurt my mother fifteen years ago, but you aren't going to get the chance to do it again."

Her eyes haunted him. They flashed and sparked; they grew dark with pain. They were familiar, all too familiar. "Laura, please." He wanted time to think, to sort out the unbelieveable thoughts racing through his mind.

"I used to dream of meeting you one day," she went on. "I used to think how wonderful it would be if we could be a family, but I was wrong."

He got to his feet and walked around to the front of the desk. "Laura, what are you saying?" He looked into those eyes that were gleaming with rage.

"I'm saying once is enough. You've hurt enough people here to last a lifetime. Go away and leave us in peace."

He knew the truth. He knew what agony twisted inside Laura and what fears drove Rachel, for the pain tearing his own heart apart could hardly be less intense. But still he couldn't truly believe it. He took Laura by the shoulders and turned her to face him. His own eyes glared back at him.

"Am I your father?" he asked.

She twisted away from his grasp as if his touch had burned her. "No! I didn't have a father until I was four and Mom married David. I didn't have anybody; neither of us did."

He felt as if he'd been kicked in the stomach. His lungs had forgotten how to breathe. Why hadn't Rachel told him? Laura's pain reflected his own and he wanted to reach out to her, to comfort the torment that was ripping through her slender frame, but he didn't dare risk her rejection again.

"Laura, I didn't know," he said quietly.

Tears were running down her face, but she didn't seem to notice. Her anger was still flowing freely. "We lived with a cousin while Mom finished high school. And what were you doing while she was trying to make us a family?" Laura's voice rang with bitterness as she mocked him in a simpering tone. "Going to college, traveling all over the world, having loads of fun."

"Laura, you've got to believe me. I didn't know."

"Mom wrote and told you."

He shook his head. "I didn't know. I would have come back if I had."

"Sure," she said sarcastically. "If you'd remembered her name."

That did it. He was hurting, but she couldn't put all the blame on him. His anger flared and he grabbed her by her shoulders again. "I would have come back in a second if I had known about you. I loved your mother. I still do."

"You don't know what love is," Laura cried. "All you know is how to hurt." She pulled away from him and ran out the door. Helen's typing slowed and stopped. The silence rang with Laura's echoing sobs until they died in the distance.

Slowly, Ben walked to the door. His steps were heavy with pain. Why hadn't Rachel told him? His uncle had known where he was all the time. She could have found him if she'd wanted to.

His steps quickened as his pain turned to anger. Why hadn't she told him? If not years ago, why not now? Surely over the last two weeks she could have found a chance if she'd wanted one.

Rather than close his office door, he went through it, past the bewildered Helen, and out into the deserted hallway.

"Dr. Healey," Helen called after him. "Your appointment. The trustees are waiting. . . ."

He let the door shut on her words. Why hadn't Rachel told him? He'd had a right to share the last fifteen years, if not with both Rachel and Laura, at least with Laura. She was his daughter.

The words both sang in his heart and drummed achingly in his brain. He had a daughter. Why hadn't Rachel told him? Damn her. Why hadn't she told him?

He was crossing the marble floor of the empty lobby of the administration building just as Rachel was hurrying in through the ornate double doors. "Oh, Ben," she cried when she saw him.

"Have you seen—" She stopped. Her face fell. "Laura's been here already, hasn't she?"

Why didn't you tell me? But the question remained a silent rhythm in his mind. He would wait; he would let Rachel explain. "She was here a few minutes ago," he said. "She dropped a bomb and then left."

Rachel's gaze scarched his face, but he kept it impassive. He'd always been good at hiding his feelings, from everyone but Rachel, that is. She didn't seem to read his turmoil though. "Was she upset?" she asked.

"Let's say the feeling was mutual."

"Oh, Ben." She touched his hand, begging for his warmth, his understanding, but he could say nothing. Slowly she pulled her hand away.

"Did she say where she was going?" Rachel asked. She looked at him with concern, then around the deserted lobby.

He shook his head. He could see her fear, could see she was torn between going after Laura and talking to him. But he couldn't say the words. Rachel had the power to bring them all together, to make them a family, but she had to make the choice.

"Ben, I have to find her," she said. "She's only a kid and she was so upset. . . ."

"I understand," he said slowly. And he did suddenly. Rachel did not need him. She hadn't needed him in the past when she discovered she was pregnant, and she didn't need him now to help her find her daughter. Their daughter. She would do it alone as she had chosen to do so much. He said nothing as she hurried back out the doors.

He just turned and walked slowly to his office. There was one final gift he could give them before he left her alone as she wanted to be.

"Get me George Wickersham," he told Helen.

Rachel flew down the administration building steps. She had made the right decision, she told herself. The only decision. She loved Ben desperately, but Laura was her child. Whatever Laura had done, she had done it because she was hurting, because she was confused and upset. And Laura was all those things because her mother had thought she could play around with the truth until it suited her to admit it.

Why hadn't she told Laura about Ben when Laura had asked on the trip up here? Why hadn't she told Laura when she had discovered Ben was indeed around? In trying to spare those she loved most, she had left them all open to more hurt. It was only fair that she be in such agony now.

Rachel looked all over the campus. In the student union, behind the tennis courts, between the stacks in the library. Science Hall was open, and the smell of waxed floors and detergent greeted her as she hurried up the steps. But Laura wasn't there either. The janitor hadn't seen anybody all morning. Rachel tried the Fine Arts Building and the gym and the Social Sciences Building, but they were all locked. She trudged back home, hoping against hope she'd find Laura there.

"No, I haven't seen Laura all morning," Rachel's mother said. "Not since you went out when she was in the gazebo. What's wrong, dear?"

"We had a riproaring argument," Rachel said lamely. "Could she have come in another door and you not know it?"

"I suppose."

Jessica helped Rachel search the house. No Laura. But their search woke up Rachel's father from his nap. He came out into the upstairs hallway to see what they were doing.

"What's wrong?" he asked.

"Laura and Rachel had a few words," Jessica said, "and Laura's gone off to pout. You just go back to your nap, dear."

Rachel was tired of all the lies, of all the half-truths and deception. Laura knew and Ben knew. Soon everyone else would know too.

"Laura found out that Ben is her father," she said.

Stunned silence swallowed them up. Her parents stared at her and the only sound for the longest moment was the ticking of the grandfather clock at the foot of the stairs.

"She wasn't happy about it," Rachel added. Her words broke the spell.

"It was that Healey fellow?" her father shouted. "That son of a—" His anger was as great as it had been the day she'd told him she was pregnant. "And now he's got the nerve to come traipsing back here as if nothing had happened!"

"Dad, he didn't know," Rachel said quickly, regretting her honesty already. She put her hand on his arm, hoping her touch could ease his rage. "By the time I wrote to him at college, he'd quit and joined the Marines."

"That no good—"

"Robert!" Jessica's voice was sharp. "What matters now is finding Laura." She turned back to Rachel, her eyes soft with sympathy. "Have you looked everywhere? Did you try the Forresters?"

"No, I forgot all about them." Laura hadn't seemed that close to the two girls, but that had to be where she was.

"I'll go call," Jessica said, and hurried downstairs to the kitchen.

Rachel was left alone with her father. She cast an uneasy glance at him, then looked down at the floor.

"I should wring his worthless neck," Robert muttered.

She was through hiding, Rachel decided, either the truth or her gaze. She met her father's eyes squarely. "Dad, it was as much my fault as his. I knew what I was doing. And as hard as those first years were, I wouldn't do a thing differently if I had the chance. I love Laura too much."

"I should have—"

"The Forresters haven't seen her today," Jessica said as she rejoined them. She gave her husband a quick glare that silenced his bitter mutterings, then turned back to Rachel. "She must have left the campus."

Lord, she could be anywhere, Rachel thought. Dubuque wasn't that big, but it was big enough. She pressed her hands against her cheeks, trying to force herself to think. Where would Laura go? Would she just wander around aimlessly, or was there someplace she would run to? Her mind stayed blank.

"I'll take the car and drive around," she said. "Maybe I'll catch a glimpse of her."

"We'll wait here," her mother promised.

But after a half hour of fruitless driving, Rachel was only more frantic. Where could Laura have disappeared to? She'd been in town only a few times; there weren't that many places she was familiar with. Just the campus, the downtown area, and Eagle Point Park. Of course, Rachel realized suddenly. That was where Laura would go.

Rachel was up near the north end of town and turned her car toward the park, half expecting to find Laura at the lookout point where they had stopped that first day. She wasn't there, but rather than leave, Rachel got out of the car. Laura was here, she knew it. She walked slowly along the path that followed the river, passing families picnicking and sightseers watching the locks below. Memories tugged at her, wanting to distract her, wanting to fool her into thinking her lies and her hidden truths hadn't really hurt anyone. She knew better though.

The path forked and she took the one that turned inland, skirting a covered picnic shelter and several barbecue pits. Up a hill and down a steep slope and she was there. The grotto where she and Ben had hidden all those years ago. And she wasn't alone. Laura was sitting on the stone wall, her head buried on her knees as she cried.

Rachel sat down next to her, putting her arms gently around Laura's shoulders. "Hi, honey."

Laura looked up, her beautiful tiger eyes awash in tears. When she saw Rachel wasn't angry, she threw herself into her mother's arms, the tears flowing anew.

"I'm sorry, Mom," she sobbed. "I was awful."

Rachel held her tightly. "I haven't been too spectacular myself lately," she said.

"I should have let you tell him." An extra-long sniffle followed.

"I had a lot of chances, honey." She brushed Laura's hair back from her forehead with long smooth strokes. "A lot of chances. I ran away from them all."

"No, you didn't. You wrote to him when you knew you were pregnant."

Rachel smiled at Laura's staunch defense of her. "But he never got the letter. I thought he had gone to Dartmouth, but I found out last week that by the time I wrote he had quit school and joined the Marines."

The sounds of the forest surrounded them for a moment. Birds chirping, the wind in the leaves.

"Why didn't you write through his relatives?" Laura asked.

"Ben's uncle worked for your grandfather, and I was scared to give a letter to Ben to anybody who knew me."

"Did you think Grandpa would open your letters?"

Rachel laughed. "I don't know that I thought anything, honey. I was just scared."

Again the silence claimed them as Laura straightened and tried to ease her tears. "Is Ben mad?"

"I don't know, but he has a right to be," Rachel admitted. "I sure made some whopping mistakes along the way."

Laura wiped the tears from her cheeks with her arm. Rachel handed her a handkerchief.

"How did you find out?" she asked, once Laura's sniffling was under control.

The girl shrugged. "I don't know. His eyes at first. Then you'd said my father had spent the summer here visiting relatives and that's what he said. He knew Grandpa didn't want you to date. Lots of little things." Laura wouldn't meet Rachel's eyes, but traced her finger over the rough edge of the stones.

"But if you knew," Rachel asked, "why did you dislike him so? You'd been talking about wanting to find him."

Laura didn't say anything for a long time. The laughter of children playing somewhere beyond the trees floated around them. Birds called and sang. A squirrel grew bold and raced past the grotto and up a tree.

"He didn't know me," Laura finally said. "It sounds stupid, but I wanted him to know I was his daughter." Her voice was little and afraid, a child calling for help.

"How would he though?" Rachel asked. "You knew I'd never reached him."

"I knew he was my father." Laura's voice grew slightly louder. A hint of belligerence trailed in the air. "He should have known me."

"Oh, Laura." Rachel pulled her daughter back into her arms amid fresh sobs. But whose sobs were they? The forest blurred and Rachel closed her eyes. "That doesn't make sense."

"I know. But I wanted it so bad." Laura sniffled loudly. "And then, when he didn't, when all he talked about was the traveling he did and the fun he'd had, I got mad. He didn't care at all." A new bout of crying began and Rachel just held her.

"Honey, he didn't mean to hurt you," Rachel said. "There really was no way he could have known. I had woven too many lies to protect us."

"I know. I really did. At least, my head knew."

Rachel laughed. "I guess that's like my head knowing I had to tell both you and Ben the truth, but the rest of me just not knowing how."

"I sure solved that problem for you," Laura said.

Rachel laughed again as sunshine once more filled her heart. She gave Laura a hug, then they both stood up. "Funny you should come here," Rachel said, gazing around the cavelike grotto. It looked more dirty and uncomfortable than romantic. "This is where Ben and I used to come."

"I know."

Rachel stared at her. "Your memory can't be that fantastic."

"Mom," Laura said with a fourteen-year-old's normal impatience. "It was the one place in the park Ben mentioned. It wasn't too hard to figure out."

"Oh." Rachel put her arm around Laura's shoulders and they started back to the car. "I can see I'm going to have to be a lot more careful about what I say around you."

Laura just laughed. They got in the car and drove home in weary, teary silence, but just before they went in the house Laura hesitated.

"Do Grandma and Grandpa know?" she asked.

Rachel nodded.

"Was Grandpa mad?"

Wasn't this what she had hoped to avoid, Rachel asked herself, that fearful, wary look in her daughter's eyes? But all she could do was nod again. "Yes, he was pretty upset," she admitted.

There was nothing to be gained by waiting though, so with a smile that promised Laura love no matter what happened, Rachel opened the back door.

"Rachel. Is that you?" Her mother came hurrying into the kitchen. "Did you find—"

She saw Laura standing timidly behind Rachel, and swept the child into her arms. "Land sakes, you gave us a scare. What in the world were you thinking of, young lady, to run off like that?" But all the while Jessica was scolding Laura, she was hugging the girl tightly, tears streaming down both their faces.

"Jess, did Rachel find her?"

Laura pulled slowly away from her grandmother as her grandfather came to the kitchen door. The air throbbed with painful silence as Laura stared at the old man. His eyes were dark, but Rachel couldn't tell if it was with anger or pain.

Twelve

"Please don't hate me, Grandpa," Laura said. The dam broke and tears again flowed down her face, creating new rivers on the dirt-streaked cheeks.

Robert reached out and clutched Laura to himself. Her little-girl sobs were lost in his shirtfront.

"I don't hate you, honey," he said. "I don't hate anybody."

A new storm of tears appeared on all fronts, but, as much as her father's understanding meant to her, Rachel had to talk to Ben. She had to make sure he also understood.

"Mom," she started, only to be stopped by the ringing of the doorbell and the phone at the same time.

Her mother grinned wryly at her, and went for the phone. Rachel went to the door. She recognized the graying old man as the head of the college's board of trustees. "Mr. Wickersham, come in," she said.

"Rachel, good to see you. Is your father available? I hate to bother him, but it's quite important."

Rachel nodded, confused by the obvious urgency in his voice. "Yes, of course. I'll get him." She started to lead the older man into her father's office, then stopped. It was Ben's office now. She escorted Mr. Wickersham into the parlor, still furnished but stripped of the small homey touches. "It'll be a few minutes," she said, and hurried back to the kitchen.

The tears had stopped and Laura and her grandparents were all holding hands. They looked up when Rachel entered.

"Mr. Wickersham wants to see you, Dad. He says it's urgent."

Robert looked surprised, but pulled Laura with him. "Where I go, my family goes."

Rachel and her mother trailed along after them. "That was Ben on the phone," Jessica told Rachel under her breath.

Rachel stopped. "Did he want to talk to me?"

Her mother shook her head, her eyes revealing her empathy for Rachel. "He just wanted to make sure we'd found Laura. He was worried too."

Rachel swallowed her pain and nodded. Of course he would have worried. She and her mother entered the parlor.

If Mr. Wickersham thought it strange that he was speaking to a group rather than one person, he gave no sign. His message was brief and to the point. "Dr. Healey's resigned," he said. "Effective immediately."

"What!" Rachel cried.

"Does that mean he's quitting?" Laura asked.

Mr. Wickersham nodded. "He's turning the presidency back over to you, Robert."

"But Grandpa doesn't want it!" Laura said.

Her grandfather frowned at her, but the love never left his eyes. "I can speak for myself, young lady. I'm not completely over the hill yet." He turned back to George. "I don't want the job. I know better than anybody all that it entails and I couldn't handle it anymore. I just hated being put out to pasture."

"Dr. Healey felt that the board wanted you back and he should step down for the good of the school," George said. "I tried to talk him out of it, but he was determined. It was time to move on, he kept saying."

"It's my fault, Grandpa," Laura whispered, sounding on the verge of tears again.

"Don't be silly," he scolded her.

Laura was being silly, Rachel knew. If it was anybody's fault, it was hers. She should have told Ben the truth weeks ago, if not years ago. If anybody had any undoing to do, it was her.

"I'll go talk to him," she said. They all turned to look at her as she rose slowly to her feet. "He's what the college needs." What she and Laura needed. "I'll make him understand that."

Brave words, but just how was she to do that? Rachel wondered as she walked across the campus. The administration building was silent. Her footsteps rang in the empty lobby as she walked across the marble floor to his office. It was dark and silent, deserted. She retraced her steps and went to the dormitory she knew Ben had taken temporary residence in. It too seemed deserted, but when she opened the door to the first floor rooms, she heard noises at the end of the hall. He was there.

Somehow her courage kept her feet moving. Closer and closer to Ben's room, even though she hadn't figured out a word of what she would say to him. She stopped at the door to the counselor's apartment. He was in the bedroom beyond the sitting room. Her feet moved her another few steps.

"Hi," she said.

He was packing and only briefly glanced her way. "Hello."

"Ah, we're being civilized," she said, and walked just into the bedroom. The furniture was sterile and bland, dormitory furniture with no personality. No trace of Ben's brief stay.

"Why not be civilized?" he asked, bitterness in his every word, his every movement. "This is a civilized age we live in, isn't it?"

He dumped a pile of loose socks on the bed next to his suitcase and stupidly, tears came to her eyes. He had nobody to take care of him, nobody to belong to, nobody to sort his socks. She remembered his loneliness, his feeling of isolation in the past, and her pain doubled. She hadn't meant to, but she had hurt him where he was most vulnerable.

"Ben, I'm sorry," she said simply, but his back stayed turned. He walked into his bathroom and she heard the clanking of bottles as he cleaned out his toiletries.

She bit her lip, searching for the magic words, the words that would make him understand. None appeared, and she reached into the pile of socks for two matching ones. She folded them together, then paired up another set.

"What the hell are you doing?" he snapped.

She looked up. He was back, his hands filled with shaving lotions and soap. His tiger eyes were blazing with anger and no hint of love.

"Your socks," she said. She matched up another pair, but he grabbed them from her hands.

"Will you stop that?" he shouted, and threw the whole pile of socks across the room. They landed in a tumbled heap at the closet door. "Just leave the damn things alone, will you? I don't need them paired up. I don't want them paired up. I hate things all neat and tidy and in sets."

His anger died as suddenly as it exploded, and in the ensuing silence they stared into each other's eyes. His were raw with pain, and he finally tore his gaze away to sink onto the bed, his head in his hands.

"Why didn't you tell me?" he cried.

"I tried," she said. His agony was tearing her apart, but her voice was quiet and almost in control. "I wrote to you at school as soon as I was sure I was pregnant, but I never heard from you."

He looked up at her. "I wasn't there anymore."

She shrugged. She walked over to the window, where she could call on the serenity of the campus to ease her turmoil. Reliving those days of fear and hurt, retelling them for Ben, brought too much of the pain back. She clenched her hands, willing the tremor from her voice.

"I know that now," she said. "But back then . . . Well, I didn't know what to think." The laughing water of the fountain just below the window mocked her, and she turned back around. "All I knew was that you hadn't answered. Had you gotten the letter but thrown it away unread? Had you read it but didn't care?"

"I would have come back if I had known!"

"I know that now, but then I didn't."

"You should have contacted me through Uncle John."

She nodded. "I know that too now."

He sprang to his feet. "Oh, come on," he snapped. "You weren't that dumb when you were sixteen. You just didn't want to bother with me!"

"For God's sake, Ben," she shouted back. "I was sixteen. I was pregnant and scared out of my mind. As far as I was concerned, you'd turned your back on me. You never wrote, you never got in touch with me. I didn't know what to do."

He sighed, running his fingers through his hair as he turned away. "That doesn't explain your silence now," he said. His voice was calmer, but the thread of tension was still pulled tight. "Why didn't you tell me sometime during the last two weeks?"

She swallowed hard, staring at her hands, the fingers woven together. "I tried," she said slowly. "Every time we were together, it was all I could think about. Should I tell you? How should I tell you? But then Father was so bitter toward you and there were the problems with the board, and the time never seemed right."

"The time never seemed right," he repeated mockingly. "So you cheated me out of more time with my daughter."

"I cheated us all, Ben. We all suffered from my decision. You, me, Laura."

He turned to face her. His eyes, his voice, were sharp. "But not David."

Rachel loved Ben, but there were limits to what she would allow. "Don't," she said. "David was good to us. I don't know if we could have made it without him. Hate me if you want, but don't hate him. Don't blame him for my mistakes."

Ben sighed. He leaned against his desk and stared at the pile of socks on the floor. "I don't hate him," he said quietly. He sounded weary, almost too tired to speak. "I'm glad he was there for you. I just hate the fact that I wasn't. That he had the chance to do for you and Laura what I would have wanted to do."

He bent down and scooped up the socks, tossing them into his open suitcase. The action had meaning for her, a terrifying meaning.

"You're not still thinking of leaving, are you?" she asked. Her mouth was a desert of fear.

"What would be the point of staying? Laura hates me, you don't need me, and the college wants your father. Seems pretty clear-cut to me." He jerked open a dresser drawer and pulled out a pile of neatly folded shirts.

"Those aren't the real reasons," she said. The desk chair was convenient and she sank into it. Her legs were no longer able to support her trembling body. "You're leaving because you can't forgive me. Why don't you just admit it?"

He frowned at her as he let the shirts fall onto the bed. "Forgiveness isn't the issue," he said.

"The real point is that you don't need me. You never have and you never will."

She got to her feet. "Ben, that's not true. I love you."

"You don't need me."

He turned away again, packing the shirts into the case, not interested in the tears that had started down her cheeks. She wiped them away impatiently. "You know that's not true. I've never been happier than I have been these last two weeks with you."

"But you don't need me." After the shirts were in the case, he started fitting in the toiletries. "When you didn't know where Laura was, you went off to find her yourself. You didn't ask me to help. You just went yourself."

"But I'm used to doing things alone."

"That's what I mean." He closed the suitcase, locked the clasps, then set it on the floor next to the bed. Another case was already there. He really was planning to go.

"So this is it?" she asked. The damn tears were starting again, but she ignored them. "You're just going to walk out on me and Laura again?"

"I'd like to stay in touch with Laura, not that she'll want me to. Maybe I can help out financially if nothing else."

"Sure, absentee fatherhood is very popular these days."

His look was bitter. "It was your choice."

"But now it's yours. Now you're the one choosing to leave me and her and the school."

"Laura won't mind." He opened the closet. It was empty except for a pair of shoes on the floor.

He stuffed them into a duffel bag. "She'd probably be willing to help me load my car."

"You're wrong. She needs you. She was hurt because you couldn't see that she was your daughter."

He grabbed up his clock and his desk lamp and put them in the duffel bag. "And what about the college? I suppose you're going to tell me that the board took another vote and wants me after all."

"My father doesn't want the job."

Ben turned to frown at her in disbelief.

"He just didn't want to leave," she added, "but he admits he can't handle all the responsibilities anymore."

Ben sighed, a deep, weary, painful sigh. "It's just not going to work," he said. "If I thought for a second that you loved me and needed me even a fraction of how much I want and need you, I'd stay."

For the first time, Rachel felt a glimmer of hope warm her. "You admit that you love me?"

"Of course I love you," he said, almost impatiently. "I've loved you all along. That's why it's hurt so much to find out you don't need me."

"Then how can you be happy if you leave?"

"How can I be happy staying and not being a part of your life?"

She wanted to scream in frustration, to shake the man and force him to believe that she loved him. "Ben, we're going around in circles."

But he wasn't listening. He zipped up the duffel bag and took a last look around the room. She had to stop him. If she didn't do something, he was going to take those suitcases and walk out that door. His car keys were lying next to her on the desk. She grabbed them.

"Let's not play games, Rachel," he said, and held his hand out.

"I'm not going to lose you again," she told him, and turned to the window. With an easy push, the screen slid open. She leaned out and tossed the car keys out the window.

"Rachel!"

The keys landed with a satisfying splash in the middle of the fountain, between Truth and Knowledge.

"That's not changing a thing," Ben informed her, and stomped from the room.

"I love you," she called, racing down the hall after him. Her voice echoed through the emptiness, but it didn't slow him down. "I need you and so does Laura. You aren't escaping so easily this time, Benjamin Healey."

He could move faster on the tiled floor than she could in her sandals. By the time she reached the fountain, he had his shoes and socks off and was rolling one trouser leg up over his knee.

"I'd forgotten how cute your legs were," she said with a giggle.

He glared and rolled up his other pant leg. She kicked her sandals off and climbed into the fountain before he had a chance. The water was warm, the bottom slippery. She moved with caution.

"What are you going to do this time?" he asked. "Swallow the keys?"

She grinned. "That's a thought!" There was no answering smile from him.

She waded along, her gaze searching the bottom for the keys. But Ben was in the water also and looking just as determinedly. She had to find those keys first.

"This is stupid, you know," he muttered as he inched along the bottom.

"You do look rather silly," she said. Dress shirt and tie, suit pants rolled up. "But cute."

"Rachel," he warned.

Her eye caught something a few feet from Honor and she hurried toward it.

"It's the keys," he said. "You see them, don't you?"

He was coming toward her. Outside of swallowing the stupid things, how could she keep him from getting them? she wondered. They were too big to swallow, so she did the only thing she could think of—she sat on them. Water swirled around her chest and poured onto the back of her neck from Honor's urn as she watched Ben approach.

"Rachel, give me the keys," he demanded.

"Take them if you want them."

"Rachel." He was eyeing her uneasily, as if he didn't trust her.

She smiled innocently at him. "I admit I'm sitting on them. If you want them, just take them from me and go."

He moved closer, clearly not trusting her. One step, two steps. He was almost next to her. He took another step and reached down with one hand. She grabbed his hand and pulled. His feet slid on the slippery bottom, skidding out from underneath him. He fell down in front of her, his hands breaking his fall, but his face and chest getting soaked. Water splashed all over her. Strands of hair plastered themselves to her forehead, but she was smiling.

"Hi," she said as he came up sputtering.

"Rachel, what's the purpose of this?" he asked. He was drenched, but didn't sound as upset as he might have considering his suit was most likely ruined, his tie was definitely looking the worse for wear, and Truth was emptying her urn on his shoulder. But the water seemed to have washed away his anger and hurt.

"You know what happens to people who wade together in the fountain," she whispered.

A small smile crept onto his lips. "We aren't wading."

"We've gone beyond that, so we must be beyond falling in love."

His eyes looked sad and she got to her knees, moving in closer to him.

"Ben, I love you," she said, framing his face with her hands. "I've made some mistakes in the past, but you are everything to me. I can't imagine living without you. Before we met again, I treasured the parts of you I saw in Laura—her eyes, the way she'd stubbornly fight to the death over some little thing, the set of her jaw. Just loving her was loving you. But now, now that I've found you again, I can't be happy with just those memories. I need to have you with me, in me, next to me."

He slowly rose to his feet. His expression was subdued. "I wish I could believe that. I'd give everything I own to be able to believe you."

She sprang up out of the water, fists clenched at her side. "Damm it, Ben. I'm taking you to meet my parents like you always demanded. What else do you want?"

Suddenly his eyes lit up and a smile spread across his face. He put his arms around her. "I don't know right now," he said. "But I'll think of something."

"Don't push your luck, buddy," she murmured, but she was smiling with satisfaction as she pulled his head to hers.

Their lips met and his arms encircled her, pulling her against him. She was in heaven, she had reached paradise. His mouth was love itself, his touch whispering promises of the happiness they'd share, of the wonder that would always be theirs.

"I don't know, Grandpa," a voice intruded. "I think it's pretty shameful myself. I thought the fountain was off limits for wading."

Rachel and Ben pulled apart, but only slightly. Their arms refused to let go of each other as they turned to see Laura and her grandfather watching them. Rachel felt Ben stiffen slightly. She could sense his worries. Her hand slid down to take his as they waded in silence to the edge of the fountain.

"Dad, have you met Ben Healey?" Rachel asked. "He's the new president of the college."

Her father nodded solemnly, as if they were meeting at a formal luncheon and Ben wasn't dripping wet. He extended his hand and Ben shook it.

"I'm pleased to meet you and honored to be taking your place," Ben said.

"So you've given up this nonsense of leaving?" Robert asked, staring directly at Ben. "Mind you, I wouldn't object to teaching a class or two, and I've got some programs I'd like to keep an eye on, but I'm too old to be thinking up new ways to sell this place to students."

"I'm sure we can work something out to keep everyone happy," Ben said.

Rachel touched his arm and they turned to Laura. "Laura," Rachel said softly. "Laura, this is your father."

Laura didn't say anything for the longest time. She just stared into Ben's eyes. She had put her glasses on, so it was blue-green tiger eyes looking into blue-green tiger eyes. Rachel saw both embarrassment and nervousness on her daughter's face, and something else too. Hope? Worry? Make it all right, Ben, she silently told him. Say something to make Laura know it's all right.

But Laura spoke first. "I'm sorry about the stuff I said earlier," she said quietly, a strange glint in her eyes. "The thing is, I get out of hand a lot. Mom has trouble keeping me in line."

"Laura!" Rachel protested. "That's not true."

Laura ignored her. "I think she needs help raising me."

"Are you sure, Laura?" Ben asked. "Are you sure you want me to stay?"

She nodded. "To tell the truth, I'm having trouble keeping Mom in line. I'm the one that needs help."

"Laura." Rachel laughed, but Ben just hugged her.

"I understand completely," he told Laura. "She threw my car keys in here and still hasn't given them back."

"They're in the fountain?" Laura exclaimed. "Can I look for them?"

"I think it's time for me to leave," Rachel's father said, laughing. "I have my reputation to uphold."

"Grandpa!" Laura said with sudden doubts, but he just pushed her gently toward Ben and Rachel.

"Your grandmother and I have some new thinking to do. You keep your parents out of our hair for a while." He kissed Laura's cheek, love shining in his eyes. Then he turned to them all. "Remember, we're expecting you for dinner. Dry, that is."

Laura had climbed into the fountain with Ben's help, and he smiled at the older man. "We'll be there." He put one arm around Rachel and the other around Laura. His gaze, too, embraced them both as his words surrounded them. "Nobody's going anyplace. This family's home."

THE EDITOR'S CORNER

I'm really impressed with the talent so many of you display for writing heart-wrenching letters! I get a lot of them about how long you have to wait for good reading between groups of LOVESWEPTs. For all of you who feel that way—and especially those of you who've written to me—I have a special FLASH bulletin. On sale right now is a fabulous novel that I believe you will want to read immediately. It's from Bantam (of course!) and is titled **WILD MIDNIGHT**. It's written by a wonderfully talented and versatile author named Maggie Davis. For a long time I've had a hunch that many women would enjoy as much as I a tale combining a number of elements: fiery sensuality, thoroughly up-to-date gothic elements in a completely believable context, and—most of all—primary characters one can really care about and root for. Trouble was, no one was writing such a book. Then along came Maggie Davis. **WILD MIDNIGHT** has thrills and chills, twists and turns galore, and a wonderfully torrid and touching romance between two unforgettable lovers. Grab a copy while you can!

As always, we're delighted to bring you a brand-new talent: Susan Richardson. Susan's first published novel is **FIDDLIN' FOOL**, LOVESWEPT #186. When an utterly charming Scottish rogue and accomplished fiddler, Jamie McLeod, performs in Sarah Hughes's hometown, he manages to turn her world upside down! His music is as wild, free, and utterly mesmerizing as the man himself. Sarah is captivated—but still part of her holds back, not believing the magic between her and Jamie could ever last. You'll be as enchanted as Sarah when Jamie sets out to woo her with thrilling music and sweet seduction.

A long time ago I read that Louisa May Alcott said that when she wrote she was "swept into a vortex" from which there was no escape (not even for sleeping or eating) until her tale was put on paper. Now, Iris

(continued)

Johansen tells me she doesn't write in the way that Ms. Alcott did, but the effect for the reader certainly is one of being "swept into a vortex." And nowhere is that storytelling power of Iris's more evident than in LOVESWEPT #187, **LAST BRIDGE HOME**. Elizabeth Ramsey is soon to give birth to the child of her late husband Mark, who was tragically killed in an auto accident during Elizabeth's first weeks of pregnancy. Then Jon Sandell, a stranger claiming to be Mark's best friend, moves into Elizabeth's life, ostensibly to protect her. But soon she realizes that her heart, her soul, belong to Jon and that the jeopardy he has told her she's in is very real indeed. This marvelous, complex love story—full of surprises—is one that I bet you'll never forget.

Again, it is a real delight for us to be able to introduce a new writer. Becky Lee Weyrich publishes her first contemporary romance novel with us. (You may have seen some of Becky's exciting long historical novels on bookracks in the last couple of years.) Becky debuts in **DETOUR TO EUPHORIA**, LOVESWEPT #188, a dilly of a book that's set in a small town in Georgia. From Sibyl Blanchard's arrest by the local sheriff to her near cardiac arrest over the charms of local lawyer Nick Fremont, who comes to bail her out, **DETOUR TO EUPHORIA** is a straight road into delightful romance. Nick brings Sibyl to his family's plantation house, and she feels as though she's stepped into a dream . . . until the time for her appearance in court draws near, and with it the end of her detour into Nick's arms. We predict you're going to grow very fond of each and every one of the wildly, wonderfully Southern (and infinitely believable) characters in this love story . . . and that you'll never forget a little Georgia town named Euphoria.

Be prepared to chuckle . . . and cheer . . . and be downright enchanted by Kay Hooper's **IN SERENA'S WEB**, LOVESWEPT #189! This is "vintage" Kay telling the story of Serena Jameson, who has the look of

(continued)
(continued)

an angel, the sexiness of a true temptress, and the devilish determination of Satan himself. Why, Serena can be nothing short of ruthless when she makes up her mind to get something and there's a wee obstacle or two in the way! Poor Brian Ashford! You have to feel just a little bit sorry for the handsome industrialist as he gets drawn into our heroine's web. He even thinks *he's* protecting *her*—from playboy Joshua Long, among others. Then Serena gets a double-whammy she richly deserves, and you'll be right on the edge of your chair as danger and desire tangle the lives of these delightful people. Be sure to pay strict attention to that rakish Joshua, because Kay isn't through with him, not by a long shot! Am I teasing you mercilessly? Just in case I am, I'll give you a sneak preview: Stay tuned for **RAVEN ON THE WING**, LOVESWEPT #193, by Kay, coming next month.

Warm wishes,

Sincerely,

Carolyn Nichols

Carolyn Nichols
  Editor
LOVESWEPT
Bantam Books, Inc.
666 Fifth Avenue
New York, NY 10103

NEW!
Handsome Book Covers Specially Designed To Fit Loveswept Books

Our new French Calf Vinyl book covers come in a set of three great colors— royal blue, scarlet red and kachina green.

Each 7" × 9½" book cover has two deep vertical pockets, a handy sewn-in bookmark, and is soil and scratch resistant.

To order your set, use the form below.

ORDER FORM